Running on Empty

JAMES H WAGGONER

writing is a joyful freedom

ISBN: 978-0-692-83266-0
LCCN: 2017901107

DEDICATION

To Blanche M. & James R.I could think of a fun childhood memory for the rest of my living days and not one would ever be the same.

To My Children, each day you do something amazing that makes me proud to say I'm your dad. Keep up the great work.

To God, whom all blessings flow, without your unselfish love and guidance none of this would be possible. To my family and friends, you are the greatest and I appreciate all of your support. Each of you has your own unique way of challenging me and keeping me grounded. To my editor, you're missed but not forgotten. I know you're up in Heaven having a great time with the other Angel editors. Thank you for sharing your years of experience and brutal review.

PROLOGUE

I listened closely and only heard one set of footsteps approaching. I raised my handgun and pointed it at the door. The footsteps stopped and the prolonged silence permeated my soul like acid corroding the top of a Die Hard car battery. I loosened my grip around my handgun and exhaled; then tightened it again and relaxed my shoulders with the barrel still pointed at the door. The sound of the door knob turning gave me a rush and I braced myself to see who was on the other side of the door.

Maison slowly walk through the door. He was wearing a dark suit with a white shirt and red tie. His smile immediately annoyed me. He stopped just inside the room and began clapping.

"You are good, Lance." he said.

I held my position and didn't respond. Maison's clapping came to an abrupt end as he stood by the entrance for a few seconds, then he walked in a little further and starting talking.

"So you just couldn't score another touchdown?" Maison asked.

The room remained dead silent. Then I saw Kyler raise his head slowly as Maison continued.

"A touchdown would have covered the spread and made everyone happy. But you had gotten so deep in debt and hooked on coke that you lost sight of what was important." Maison shouted.

Kyler in his beaten state coughed and mustered up enough vocal strength to respond.

"Maison?" he asked as he coughed.

"Yea it's me, you worthless bastard." Maison said.

Kyler started laughing and soon the laughter turned to sobs and tears.

"I wish I had never met you. Your smooth talk and lavish parties ruined my career." Kyler said.

"Bullshit! You were a grown-ass man. No one twisted your damn arm. You put me in a bad place with a lot of people." Maison said.

"You're a joke. That was five years ago. Is that why you have this coward torturing me?" Kyler said.

Maison didn't respond and it appeared that the dialogue between the two old acquaintances was over. I looked at Maison but he had his head down looking at the floor. Kyler was sitting in the chair laughing. I guess being the outsider I missed the joke because I didn't see anything funny. Kyler had been a better-than-average football player at some point, I'm assuming, if Maison gambled on his talent. I'm not sure how the relationship became estranged besides the drug use and the typical athlete's mentality towards money. But I wasn't a psychiatrist and really didn't give a damn. Kyler's life was coming to an end soon and my relationship with the real estate tycoon would be over soon thereafter. I still hadn't heard from Catalina, which worried me to no end. I didn't know if Thad's flunky cop associates had gotten to her or she was not talking to me because of the danger I had put in. Maybe she had resigned and left me a note on the kitchen counter. My mind raced at galactic speed thinking of all the possible outcomes. Unfortunately, I couldn't wrap my head around one. Thad had been arrested. I didn't know what Kennedy had told the feds. Bottom line is I had to wrap up this little reunion and get someplace safe so I could get my thoughts together. I yelled Maison's name and he looked up, startled.

"Are you done reminiscing?" I asked.

Maison smiled before he replied.

"Of course, I am. I take it you're ready to get paid?" Maison asked. In my current mental state I didn't have time for his apparent amusement. I raise the 9mm to Kyler's right temple and he shied away. He was begging, pleading with me not to kill him. I saw Maison's smile get as wide as a new four-lane road extension. We stared at each other in silence for a few seconds. I looked at the beaten jock, took one last look at Maison before the sound of a single round shattered Kyler's brain onto the floor and broke the silence. Maison stood there still smiling, now clapping before he spoke.

"Well done." he said.

I didn't respond. His validation as a clean hands high-paying murderer didn't mean a damn thing to me. I still had the gun raised and my heart was beating fast like this was my first time killing someone. I slowly lowered the gun and put it in the small of my back and started packing up my working tools. I felt the awkwardness in the room. Not that I had any emotional ties to Kyler, but something didn't feel right. I didn't look at Maison as I asked when I would get the balance of my payment. He said we had some other business to finish up. I had no idea what he was talking about. When I zipped up my duffle bag I turned and asked him "What business are you referring to?"

"What interests you, Lance, besides the obvious?" he asked.

"A little late for personal interest, don't you think?" I asked.

"Seriously! A single man; no kids; never been married. Does that get lonely?" Maison asked.

"Look Maison, our business is done. When can I get the balance, or is this when you screw me and don't pay the balance?" I asked.

He laughed and continued with his inquisition.

"I asked because I know of at least two relationships you didn't give fair chances." he said.

"And how do you know so much about me? Who are you anyway?" I asked, perplexed.

Maison didn't answer me. Instead he put his right hand in his pocket. I reached behind my back and pulled out the 9mm and pointed it at him. When he pulled his right hand out of his pocket he had a cell phone in his hand. I saw him pressing buttons, ignoring me until he was done. Then he asked me if I had been to any art galleries recently. Now I was the one with the blank look. I had no idea where he was going with the questioning. The smell of blood and brain matter invaded my nostrils as I stood facing Maison. The door by Maison flung open and what I saw instantly took away my last breath. Two heavy men walked in with two women. One was an older woman, Catalina, and the other young lady I didn't recognize but she screamed loudly and yelled out Kyler's name. Maison told her to shut her mouth and the man holding her back-handed her across the face. My eyes were fixed on Catalina. Her eyes were swollen and red. She had been crying but she didn't look physically harmed.

"What the hell is going on, Maison?" I asked with my gun pointed at him.

"Lance, what does it look like?" he asked arrogantly.

"Why do you have Catalina?" I asked.

The other lady repeated my name twice in surprise.

"Lance? Lance Goodman?" she asked.

I strained my eyes to see her clearer and couldn't believe what my eyes focused in on; it was Jordan Hughes. The last time I saw her I had just made the dreadful decision to take in two strangers in hopes that they would love me in time. My contemptuous mind led me to her job with aspirations of starting a relationship with her. Now her brother's brains were splattered on the floor by my hands.

Not exactly a great way to get reacquainted. She screamed, started kicking trying to free herself, and asked if I killed her brother. The man holding her was three times her size. Her antics unimpressed him and only frustrated her. I didn't respond to her question; the scene spoke for itself. The bigger question was, what was in this for Maison and how did he know so damn much about me?

"You see Lance...I know exactly the last time you visited an art gallery. I was there with my daughter, Sofia Gaboni. She didn't introduce us but she constantly talked about you. Is your memory coming back?" he asked.

Before I could answer, Maison told the man holding Catalina to slap her to get my attention. The brute didn't hesitate and I saw his huge hand slap her aged face. She started to cry right away and I cringed. Maison hadn't necessarily hired me just to kill Kyler. Instead he used him as a pawn in his own vendetta to avenge the death of his daughter. Sofia had kept her name from her short-lived marriage. Before she got married, she went by the name of Sofia Boutte, her mother's maiden name. She didn't go by her father's last name of Chambers.

I looked around the room for another door. This wasn't going to end well at all. My thoughts went back to the last conversation I had with Eduardo about two compact discs containing proof of corruption at the highest levels. Instead of asking for a generous reward and going about my business, my emotions had got the best of me. I tried numerous times to convince my demonic state that I was doing the right thing by saving two fatherless girls. All I did was complicate my life and theirs further. Because of many skeletons my paranoia levels were out of balance worse than the U.S. deficit. I didn't have regard for lives or freedom of those I once would have defended. I threw Thad away like a sacrificial lamb and had no idea killing Sofia Gaboni would bring my world crumbling down.

Two more men had now entered the room with weapons aimed at me. I looked at Catalina weeping and looking pitifully frail in the huge man's hands. I kept my gun lifted and aimed at Maison's temple as I began to back up. There was another door about twenty feet away. As I backed up I found myself crying and apologizing to Catalina. I told her I never meant for it to end this way. I told her I loved her and that she was the best thing to come into my life. I didn't acknowledge Jordan. She had her own issues with her dead brother. Maison with a shit-eating grin told me it was over and there was no way out. I ignored his invitation to surrender and continued to back up. Jordan called me a ruthless bastard and said that this explained the cash withdrawal and my uncanny behavior. I heard a familiar sound liven the room, but it came from an unusual direction; normally the loud sounds came from my side. I felt two bullets pierce my skin. I dropped my duffle bag and squeezed my trigger. I hit Maison in his left shoulder. I grabbed my side and the inside of my left hand revealed a dark red color. Catalina screamed as another bullet struck my body and I dropped to one knee. My gun had fallen out of my hand a few feet away. I tried to reach for it but another bullet hit my body and stopped my progress. More screams came from my Latina mother. My vision grew blurred as I slumped down onto the floor. I lay there trying to focus, but I couldn't make out anything. I felt my body temperature drop. The screams slowly faded and my eyes kept blinking quickly until I blacked out.

I don't know how long I was unconscious but when I opened my eyes my vision was still blurred. I could see a silhouette of a small-framed person down by my feet. I couldn't move though. I was in a bed I could tell that much. I tried to lift my left hand but I couldn't, it felt confined. I turned my head to the side to see my left hand handcuffed to a hospital bed rail. With the little strength I had I shook my hand but it was no use. My right hand was free and I felt something inside the palm of my hand with a button.

When I started to move, I saw the silhouette get up and come towards me. As it got closer I could see it was Catalina. She grabbed the handcuffed hand and started rubbing it. Catalina told me I was at Martin Luther King Hospital but the authorities were outside the door. I could hear her saying something else but I couldn't make it out, I did hear my friend's name Townsend. Then I saw two dark silhouettes rush into the room. As they got closer I saw their badges. It read L.A.P.D, but I couldn't make out the names. My aching ears heard sounds from both of the officers. I could hear Catalina telling them I needed to rest. They ignored her and kept shouting at me. I thought I heard one of the officers tell her this was a multiple homicide investigation and they had some questions for Mr. Goodman. I recognized my name and I closed my eyes. One of the officers came down to my ear and whispered, "We take care of our own, motherfucker." I felt a small blade pierce my side. My mind drifted to Thad. His life would never be the same thanks to my narcissistic ways. I thought about the other Mr. Goodman, the man who walked out of my life and never taught me about manhood or love. I wondered if he had any regrets. I wondered did he ever love my mother or was she a convenient thing until the next best thing came along. That next best thing was cocaine and heroin became the better thing. Finally, the human immunodeficiency virus ended his misery and ended my mother's hopeless love for the man who had walked out of both our lives. I pressed the self-medicating button rapidly with my right thumb to take me away from all the noise. The morphine slowly entered my bloodstream and the sounds I heard faded along with the bad childhood memories and my eyes remained closed.

RUNNING ON EMPTY

A clash of loud thunder woke me up. My body was drenched in sweat from another night of terrifying demons eating what was left of my soul. I couldn't move or even wipe the sleep from my eyes. I heard several beeps from a heart monitor. Next to the monitor were two clear tubes hanging with liquid flowing to an IV in my right arm. The room I was in wasn't my own. My left arm was handcuffed to the bed railing. I was in excruciating pain. I lay in this unknown place blinking my eyes quickly trying to remember what happened and how I got here. Nothing immediately came to the frontal. No one else was in the room with me, but from outside of the glass windowpane I could see a lot of people. A female nurse barged in with a clipboard and a tray of pills.

"Good morning Mr. Goodman," she greeted.

I opened my lips to respond but nothing came out. The nurse proceeded with what I assume was her routine medical examination and told me I was getting a little stronger every day. My eyes were fixed on her as she checked my blood pressure then my temperature before opening my mouth and shoving three pills down my throat followed by just enough water in a dingy pale yellow Dixie cup. As she washed my face I opened my mouth and tried to speak. In a low whisper I uttered, "Where am I?"

My morning visitor stopped wiping my brow. She looked towards the foot of the bed at the glass window at the dark images I couldn't make out and told me I had been arrested for doing some very bad things and that I was in a lot of trouble. My eyes got wide and my blood pressure immediately increased. I tried to shift in the bed but it was useless. My body was too weak and the handcuffs didn't help. At that moment, the door flung open and two men in dark uniforms rushed in. I heard them ask the nurse if I was conscious and her response was that I was responding in and out. The police officers told her to leave them alone with me. As soon as the nurse was out of their sight they began punching me in my aching ribs repeatedly and cursing at me. I heard the name Thad from one of the officers. I didn't recognize the name but they kept telling me I was going to pay for what I did. The goons stopped beating me when the door opened abruptly. It was a doctor who I assumed was working the evening shift.

"What's going on in here?" he demanded.

They brushed past the doctor, "Police business doc." Then slammed the door behind them. The doctor came to the side of my bed and sat down. He was an older medical professional. His hair and eyebrows were salt and slightly peppered. He was cleaned shaven and the scent of old school Lagerfeld blew past my nose. His hands showed many years of major surgeries and long ER shifts. He patted my hand and began to speak to me.

"Mr. Goodman, you've recovered quickly but I'm still not ready to release you into police custody. I don't feel you'd make it to the station." He said.

Again, a low whisper was all I could muster,

"How did I get here Doc?"

"You honestly don't remember?" he asked.

I shook my head from side to side.

"You've been arrested for murder and are a possible suspect in several other murders. The LAPD seem to have a personal interest in you." He told me.

Hearing his words sent an eerie feeling through my body. I knew the fraternity of L.A.'s finest was after me for using one of their own as a sacrificial lamb. Maison had used me worse than a $10 trick off of Figueroa. I don't remember the last time I saw Catalina or if she's even safe. The doctor continued talking to or rather at me as my mind was racing a million miles now and I was only taking in bits and pieces of what he was saying. I heard him describe my condition. I had two broken ribs, four gunshot wounds and that I suffered a serious blow to the head. He indicated I would be here at least three more days and to get as much rest as possible. When the doctor left my room I saw L.A.'s finest glaring through the glass pointing at me with evil faces. I ignored them and turned the television on. It seemed like every channel had on the news. I tuned in to Channel 4 just in time to see a news clip about none other than yours truly. A much younger picture of me was in the right corner of the screen next to a mouthy news reporter.

In the quiet town of Los Feliz Hills businessman Lance Goodman, owner of a community print shop is being accused of kidnapping and murder with a trail of blood on his hands instead of his company's ink. The suspect is currently under surveillance at Martin Luther King

Hospital. We'll keep you posted on the latest developments during the ongoing investigations.

I searched for ESPN but the only available channels were broadcasting with each reporter saying the same shit in a different way. Irritated, I hit the power button and turned off the television and lay in bed. My mind was in a tailspin. I was trying to gather my thoughts and figure out my next move. I couldn't pass the thought of Catalina and where she might be. I thought about Thad for a split second but quickly felt my head start to hurt from thoughts of the weasel minded Maison Chambers. The pain in my side returned and I hit the medication button, as the slow drips of morphine entered my body the pain faded and eventually so did I.

A loud ringing interrupted what felt like the most peaceful sleep I'd had in years. I looked to my left then to my right to see a cream colored push button phone screaming. I slid as close as I could to stop the disturbance. I picked up the receiver but didn't say anything. A few seconds went by before the other party spoke. The voice was soft and soothing but unfamiliar as they asked for me.

"Is this Lance?"

I cleared my throat and inquired as to who was calling.

They repeated their question.

"Is this Lance Goodman?"

"Yes. Who is this?" I asked.

"Oh my God, I didn't think it was true but it was you on the news."

Now I was curious and asked who was speaking?

"This is Londen, Lance. Do you remember me?" she asked.

I processed the name but couldn't place the name. Images flashed through my head quickly and I could recognize them but the name wasn't ringing a bell. I returned to the stranger on the line.

"I apologize but I don't think I know you." I said.

The line disconnected and a loud dial tone is all I heard. I placed the receiver back on the telephone base and lay in bed thinking. She did say Londen not Jordan, right? Think Lance, why would anybody call your room and play the "remember me" game? I kept playing her voice over in my head but was interrupted by the night shift nurse coming to check my vitals. She was a bubbly woman with a deep voice, a little on the heavy side, but she moved swiftly on her feet. She grabbed my arm to check the IV before checking my blood pressure and my temperature then she was gone. Soon after she left the cafeteria staff made their rounds. It was another plastic tray of Salisbury steak, lumped mashed potatoes, a salad with a half teaspoon of salad dressing, and a kid sized cup of apple juice. Not exactly the gourmet meal I'd last ordered at the BOA Steakhouse on Sunset. I took a few bites of the grizzled steak before lying back down. I dozed off watching 60 minutes. I'm not sure how long I had been asleep but I woke to the sound of a male nurse's voice. I hadn't seen him in my room before but his voice sounded familiar. He was moving quickly about the small room while LAPD started glaring through the glass again. He stood at the foot of the bed reviewing my medical chart and finally spoke.

"How are you feeling Mr. Goodman?" he asked.

I raised my head to get a better look at my latest hospital caretaker. I could see he was about 6'2" with brown skin and very fit. His scrubs weren't baggy but snug. I could see the muscle veins in his biceps. He had a small scar around his top lip.

"What time is it?" I whispered.

"1:47 AM." He replied.

He then walked to the side of my bed, lowered his voice and continued talking to me.

"Listen Lance, I'm going to get you the hell out of here but you have to be ready to roll."

The more he spoke the more recognizable his voice became. I immediately opened my eyes. He wasn't a staff member at Martin Luther King Hospital. Our bond ran much deeper. The raspy voice was my old-time buddy Townsend! I was too weak to even shake his hand. He patted my arm and continued talking to me and told me to remain calm and unassuming to not arouse any suspicion. While gazing over his shoulder, Townsend slid a three-inch scalpel into my free hand. I had a million questions for him but could only get two out of my mouth.

"How did you get here? How did you know I was in the hospital?" I asked.

Townsend spoke quickly but cautiously, keeping the medical clipboard close to his lips as he spoke. "Catalina called me and told me you had been shot several times. She wasn't sure you were going to make it and that you had been arrested."

Townsend continued to tell me he caught the first flight from John F. Kennedy International airport to LAX. When he landed, he called Catalina but my cell phone was going straight to voicemail. Like me, he had caught the story on one of the local news channels.

"No more questions. I'm going to get a wheelchair and let these rookies know you're going for a MRI." he said.

My eyes were still big and full of amazement. I didn't know if I should be thanking God or the Devil. According to the law I was in the right place until a jury of my peers decided my fate. My confused confession was interrupted.

"Lance, do you know what to do with that scalpel? He asked. I'm going to take one and you have to slice the other one." he told me.

Townsend was always swift and could make a crime scene look relentless. I nodded my head and lay back in the bed. My free hand was gripping the weapon standing between 25 to life and freedom. I heard the door close and saw Townsend talking to the men in blue. Both of the officers peeked through the glass and nodded their heads. I felt my heartbeat racing as I saw the men come into my room. The police officers looked angry. Townsend asked if I was ready for my MRI while he released the brakes on the hospital bed. I felt one of the officers elbow me in my ribs. We got to the elevator and Townsend pushed the down button and extended his phony appreciation to the officers for their service. My hand was camouflaging the scalpel as best I could.

I heard the elevator ding and saw the doors open with a blur. Inside the elevator there were shades of blue on each side of the hospital bed. Their hands were resting on the leather clip to draw their weapons. When the doors closed Townsend wasted no time and kicked one of the officers in his knee, grabbed his head and slammed his knee into his face and snapped his neck. The other officer went to draw his weapon and I cut the artery at his wrist causing him to yell out in mercy as blood splattered across my face. His gun fell to the ground and Townsend quickly moved my bed and punched him two times. He reached for the officer's handcuffs and cuffed his other hand to my bed. A pool of blood was forming on the elevator floor as we descended to the ground floor. The cop told Townsend we'd never get away with this. Townsend took the officer's Billy club and began striking him fiercely across the head until you could see the fleshy tissue just under his skin. When the elevator reached the ground floor, Townsend had a 9mm pointed at the door. The doors slowly opened and Townsend moved to the open door with the weapon pointed forward and his hand on the trigger. After he didn't see any one coming he un-cuffed the bleeding cop and pulled my bed out of the elevator and headed for the exit. I immediately felt the cool breeze of the evening across my face. I heard my friend tell me to hang in there. Just outside the hospital in the long-term parking lot, Townsend sat me up and leaned me against him in a modified firemen's carry and lifted me from the bed. I felt us moving swiftly until we reached the side of a 4-door sedan. Townsend leaned me up against the car until he could open the door. I saw him look around the parking lot. I was in so much pain. He sat me in the passenger seat up front, buckled me in and closed the door. When he got in the car he told me we had a bit of a journey to go and that we wouldn't make any stops until we got to our destination. I nodded and turned my head towards the window. I felt the car's transmission shift to drive. My ribs were killing me but I managed to hit the button to let the window down. The cool wind felt so good and it took my mind to Catalina still wondering if she was alive. Then I looked over at my friend. He was cool and collected as he drove us to the unknown location. I turned back to the window and dozed off. Just like that I was a free man again.

I was jolted awake from the slamming of Townsend's car door. We were parked in front of a stucco home with a big oval window, manicured lawn and a small dark porch. The roof was made of stacked shingles and drab in color. All of the windows had bars on them including the front door. Townsend came around to my side of the car to help get me out. My shirt was soaked with blood and my whole body ached terribly. The street was narrow and unfamiliar.

There were cars parked on both sides of this residential neighborhood. Many of the homes appeared identical and made from the same blueprint. As we got closer to the porch I saw 10488 pasted to the house in an angle up and to the right. I never thought walking up four measly steps would be so painful. Each step felt like I was going to fall even with the strength of my friend holding me up. Townsend leaned me up against the wall as he fumbled for the keys to the bar door and front door. He unlocked the bar door and I asked him,

"Where are we?"

"Compton!" He said bluntly.

Townsend opened the front door, turned on the light and helped me inside. Just a few steps inside was a small sofa. I staggered towards it, holding on to Townsend for dear life. As soon as I was in arm's distance I reached for the sofa and fell down on it. The plush looking cushion was lumpy and didn't help my pain. I was out of breath and needed to catch my wind. As I lay there on the couch, I could see what looked like the kitchen off to the side and three doors along a small hallway presumably bedrooms and at least a bathroom. Next to the sofa was a cramped opening that housed a small table with 2 chairs. Townsend must have sensed my observation.

"I know it isn't luxury accommodations, but you are alive and free." He said.

"I'm cool man." I spat back.

"Bathroom is down the hall on the left. There's a first aid kit in there. I'll have a nurse come by here later on today." He snarled.

"Thanks." I replied before attempting to stand up.

Townsend's words were lethal like venom dripping from a poisonous snake. That was Townsend though. I didn't take it personal and I knew we'd have our summit as soon as the sun stretched across the smog capital of the world. I managed to make it to the bathroom without falling again. The bathroom served its purpose. The medicine cabinet revealed only a man resided there. I found the first aid kit underneath the face bowl. The kit had been used before but I found some gauze, a few Band-Aids and a topical ointment. I caught a glimpse of myself in the mirror. The blood from my gunshot wounds had seeped through my shirt. As I lifted my shirt over my head, Townsend knocked on the door. When I opened the door he handed me two white cotton crew neck t-shirts and some shorts.

"Appreciate it!" I said.

"Towels are up there." He said pointing to the cabinet above the toilet.

Townsend walked back to one of the rooms and slammed the door. The thought of taking a shower hadn't crossed my mind. Everything happened so fast that I hadn't processed anything. I stood in the mirror looking at my wounded body trying to figure out how I was going to tell my best friend of two decades I had fucked up and thank him at the same time. I pulled the plastic shower curtain back and turned the knob on for the hot water. When I felt the water getting hot I turned on the cold water slightly and lifted the shower knob. The water came out slowly through four of the tiny outlets. I let the shower run a few minutes and took off the rest of my clothes. I opened bar of Irish Spring soap and grabbed a washcloth. The inside of tub had discoloration and some mold in the corners. The shower caddy was rusted and had an old razor and a piece of soap on it. As the water hit my body it ached, and my mind drifted once again to thoughts of Catalina. I hadn't yet had a chance to ask Townsend about her. I felt my face tightened as I had flashbacks of Maison Chambers laughing over my bullet filled body. I began rubbing the washcloth hard against my body as the image continued to flood my mind. Then I saw a gullible face smiling – Thad. I knew his fraternal law brethren weren't going to rest until I was dead or locked away for life. Preferably dead! I felt the water turning lukewarm so I finished up quickly. I stood in the mirror and applied the gauze to my injury with the tape as best I could. Before putting on one of the crew neck t-shirts, I looked for some deodorant but didn't find any. The shorts were a little snug but would have to do. When I came out of the bathroom I could hear my friend talking to someone, more like yelling at them. Townsend was behind closed doors in one of the 3 rooms in the hallway. I dared not knock on his door to inquire. I walked down the hall to the other door and opened it. Inside were a full size bed and a small stand with an older model television with the remote control resting on top. I grabbed the remote, sat down on the bed and hit the red power button. When the color tube came on, there was a newscaster reporting live from Martin Luther King Hospital.

Reports are still coming in from what looks like a gangland style escape. Just hours ago murder suspect Lance Goodman escaped. The suspect was being treated for injuries sustained during his arrest. Officials say two L.A. police officers were slain during the escape. The suspect may be armed and is considered extremely dangerous. Authorities are asking for the public's help. If you see Lance Goodman, call 911. Reporting live from Martin

Luther King Hospital, I'm Amanda Tgyuen.

The same outdated picture of me was posted in the background on the nightly news. Unable to keep my eyes open any longer, I turned off the TV and laid down. I don't know how long I had been asleep but my nose detected a fruity scent in my immediate area. I opened my eyes to see a woman sitting in a folding chair by the bedroom door. Her complexion was a light shade of brown. She didn't appear to be tall, maybe 4 ft. 5 in and on the petite side. She was dressed in a dark pair of slacks, a navy pinstripe blouse, and a dark blazer. Her shoes were leather and black with a 4 inch heel. She had on a pair of glasses and her hair was long and wavy; just past her shoulders. When she noticed that I was awake and looking at her, she stood up and introduced herself. I recognized immediately that her tongue wasn't American.

"Hi Mr. Goodman, my name is Naomi Manuelz. Mr. Townsend asked that I look after you." She said.

"Hi. What do you mean look after me?" I asked.

"I understand you have some injuries that need medical attention." She said.

"Are you a doctor?" I inquired.

"No I'm a nurse."

It was evident from the tone of Nurse Manuelz response that she was as annoyed as I was. I could barely sit up. I was in so much pain. The nurse came over to lend me a hand. I was surprised by her strong grip and that she was able to assist me. I asked her how old she was. She told me she was old enough to know my injuries were serious. She took off her blazer and pulled out what looked like a medical bag from a navy blue backpack. The white t-shirt I put on earlier was no longer white. It was stained heavily with my own blood. Naomi asked if I had another shirt to put on. I nodded. She pulled a pair of scissors from the medical bag and started cutting the shirt off of me. It hurt like hell when I raised my arms over my head and I let out a low grunt.

"Oh yes Mr. Goodman you need some help. How old are these injuries?" She asked.

"Honestly, everything is still a blur so I couldn't tell for certain." I told her.

"Don't worry I'll have you back to 100% in no time but you have to relax and not give me any attitude."

"I'll be fine!"

Naomi pushed me back on the bed and pointed her finger at me.

"Look! Townsend told me you might be feisty but not

to take any shit from you. Now I can either help you or you can keep bleeding until you die on this bed. Makes no difference to me." And she walked out and slammed the door. I lay there starring at the popcorn ceiling trying to get my thoughts together. My current situation was worse than it had ever been. I didn't know if Catalina was alive. I didn't have access to my money and let's not forget I'm a wanted man. I'm sure my home was under surveillance 24/7 by L.A.'s finest so I couldn't go there and get any of my assorted artillery.

"Naomi!" I yelled.

She stood there and asked, "Do you have a better attitude?"

"I'm sorry. I'm not used to anyone helping me."

"No excuse for you to be such an asshole."

She left the door opening without saying a word. When she returned she was holding a gold medium sized bowl. I could see a sponge under her arm. She sat the bowl by the bed, dipped the sponge inside the bowl and gently began rubbing it against my body. Her bedside manner wasn't pleasant. She still had attitude written across her forehead. When she finished she told me to sit up so she could dress my wounds with new Band-Aids. She didn't speak a word. I started to say something but thought better of it. I knew I had pissed her off. After she finished applying the gauze she asked if I needed help putting on my shirt. I told her no and she didn't acknowledge my answer instead she just walked out. Just before she walked out of the room I asked her where was she from. She stopped but didn't look at me, or answer immediately. I heard the front close. Townsend was back.

"Central America." She said and walked out.

I heard my best friend ask her if I was going to be ok. She told him yes and that I was a pain in her ass. Townsend walked into the bedroom and stared me down. Finally he said,

"Get your ass up, and let's take a ride."

I did my best to get up without making too many grunts but I was hurting like a son of a bitch. Townsend thanked Naomi and told her to come back this afternoon and that my attitude would be better. I didn't think it would but I didn't intrude on the conversation. When I got to the living room they both looked at me in disgust. I looked at them the same way and kept walking towards the front door. Standing on the porch taking in some fresh air felt good. I could hear cars and horns honking from a distance but I was still clueless as to my whereabouts. Naomi walked past me without saying goodbye and got into a black Honda 2 door coupe. Her windows were tinted dark and she had a personalized license plate that read DA BST RN. Townsend wasn't far behind her. Before he locked the door he asked if I was ready. It's not like I could say no let me grab my wallet. My silence told him that I was ready and he walked past me to the car. I walked down the four steps sideways. Each step brought on a new pain. By the time I made it to the car I was out of breath. We pulled out of the driveway and headed north. When we reached the end of the block I saw the street signs – El Segundo Blvd and Clovis Ave. Townsend made a right turn on El Segundo Blvd then another right on Central Ave. I saw a High School painted in red on the left as we zoomed down the avenue. I cracked my window for some more fresh air. Townsend couldn't hold it any longer.

"Lance, what the hell happened?"

I didn't respond. I just rode looking out the window. I knew it was coming sooner or later and he'd want answers. Answers I wasn't ready to give. I only wanted to get back on my feet and go after the person who put me in this position. Townsend continued his rant telling me I needed to get it together quickly because the streets were already talking and I didn't have a lot of time. I took it all in and blew it right back out. I knew exactly what needed to be done and he was either going to help me or take his ass back to New York and take that fruity smelling nurse with him. First things first, I needed to find out if Catalina was alive and safe.

"Have you spoken to Catalina?" I interrupted his one sided conversation.

Townsend looked at me out of the corner of his eye and said,

"Dude, she's the least of your concerns right now."

We stayed on Central Avenue until we arrived in the city of Carson. Townsend asked me how I was holding up. My pain level was excruciating but I lied and told him I was good to go. Just past the 91 Freeway we turned into a mobile home park. We stopped in front of a green mobile home. The fabricated dwelling had a shade awning and a dark blue Cadillac parked under the carport. The front door of the mobile home had a flimsy screen door hanging on by two screws and the door was open. I could see a large man sitting in a recliner watching television. Townsend got out of the car and tapped on the side of the mobile home. I heard someone yell "It's open."

"What's up Little Red?" Townsend asked.

"Another day above ground." The man said.

He wasn't little at all. I wasn't immediately introduced. Townsend told "Little Red" I was the guy he told him about.

"No shit? This is the dude Maison played?" He asked.

Townsend looked my way and nodded.

"This is the dude L.A.P.D wants dead?" He continued.

"Let's get down to business." Townsend said.

"Okay! Maison is out of the country and I'm sure he doesn't know your man is still alive but he will soon." Little Red said.

He then tossed a manila envelope over to Townsend and continued updating us. Little Red said the young rookie caught by the feds in Florida was due back in Los Angeles any day now. He had been released on bond and charged with a felony and his career as a cop was over. Little Red looked at me directly and asked,

"Are you ready to dance with the devil?"

"I've been dancing with him for a while now." I responded.

"Townsend, what's in the envelope?" I asked.

He didn't respond. He thanked the large fella and let me know it was time to leave. When we got back in the car, he pressed the envelope against my aching ribs, looked dead in my face and said handle your business Lance. It's time to end this bullshit. His look took me back to the first time we did a score together and he introduced me to his low tolerance for emotions. The target had given us what we were to collect and there was no kill contract on him. However, Townsend believed if a person did you wrong once, if given the chance they'd do you wrong again. So there were no second chances, he tied the man's wrist and ankles with zip ties and as the man lay there squirming and pleading for his life, Townsend poured gasoline on him and lit him on fire. He let the flames burn long enough to char the man. The man was barely breathing. Townsend kicked him and the man coughed. I stood there shocked at his detached feelings. Townsend knelt down and burned the man's eyes. The screams were deaf to his ears as continued punishing this helpless person. Then he stood, looked at me and asked,

"What you think Lance? You think he's learned his lesson?"

I could barely muster the words to answer.

"Yes! I'm sure he gets the message." I finally answered.

As soon as the last syllable rolled off my tongue, Townsend pulled out a 9MM handgun and pulled the trigger repeatedly until all you heard was click, click, click.

He tapped me on the shoulder as he walked by and told me it gets easier.

Townsend snapped me out of my travels down memory lane and told me I didn't have a lot of time. He continued saying I could do one of two things: appreciate that I'm free and relocate to a non-extradition country or take what's in the envelope pressed against my ribs and destroy the man who left me for dead. Either way I'd have to move smartly and quickly, no emotions, no relationships. If I needed some company, find the most expensive liar and pay her to give my ego some attention. My best friend was tough as they came. For as long as I'd known him, I couldn't recall him having a woman close to him. He didn't frequent spots often and he didn't allow too many people inside his circle. His bulletproof philosophy kept him out of the penal system; drama free in relationships and his kill rate was well respected across the fifty states and a few countries. Again, he asked me if I was listening and what was I going to do? As the car traveled down Avalon Blvd towards the 405 Freeway I slowly removed the now damp envelop from my ribs, I gazed out of the window without answering. He didn't press the issue and kept driving. We rode all the way back to Compton in silence. When we pulled into the driveway Townsend told me the nurse would be back and not to give her any problems. She was only there to help at his request. I silently acknowledged what he was saying as I walked towards the front door. Once inside I didn't stop in the tiny living room, but continued to my room and slammed the door behind me. I threw the envelope on the bed and stood there collecting my thoughts. I could barely lift my arms over my head without feeling serious pain. My mind was overloaded with an array of thoughts. The uncertainty of Catalina's whereabouts was driving me crazy. The ultimate demise of Maison caused my insides to turn just thinking how badly I was going to torture him. The retaliation anticipated from Thad really didn't trouble me. He would simply have to be killed along with anyone who helped him. I had to return to the crazed animal I once was before I thought I could buy love and affection from two fatherless kids. That person had no feelings. My lifestyle provided a source of income in exchange for a steady stream of blood; blood that could be washed away from my hands but never from my soul. I had killed so many people that there was no way anyone could ever love me and I needed to accept the same – I could never love any one. I heard a tap on the door and yelled a loud "yeah". Townsend opened the door and walked in. He had a laptop, a black duffle bag and a cell phone. He sat the items on the bed and told me the laptop was untraceable, the cell phone was a fresh burner with a SIM card and I knew what to do with the contents inside the duffle bag. I saw him look at the envelope on the bed then back at me. Then he walked out of the room and closed the door without saying another word. I sat on the bed and opened the envelope. Inside was more information on Maison Chambers than I had found. I had copies of all of his real estate ventures and the partners. Copies of his bank statements and all of the banks he was affiliated with. Inside were the addresses to 2 homes, one in Beverly Hills, CA and another in Calabasas, CA. I saw photos of a Latina woman and two small children inside as well but the woman wasn't Sofia. I didn't know if the female was his wife or a girlfriend. The kids really threw me for a loop because I didn't find any of this information about him when I did my background check. I turned each picture over to see if there was any writing on the back. The name Rosalie Contreras was scribbled on the back along with the writing 'longtime mistress'. The photo of a boy had the name Micah written. Scribbled by his name were the words 'Maison's son by Rosalie' age 10. The bottom of both photos said Omaha, NE with an address. The whole scenario played like an old vinyl album in my ears. But I knew this time around to leave the playing field empty and not allow my emotions to get involved. My emotions were partly the blame for the shit storm I was currently in. I threw the pictures on the bed and unzipped the duffle bag. Inside there were two 9mm handguns with several rounds of ammunition, a foreign made automatic rifle and lastly I saw ten stacks of $10k wrapped in plastic. Because of an overzealous young cop and nosey art dealer my life had been reduced to a full sized bed, a duffle bag of illegal firearms and the only money I had was the tightly wrapped bills. I looked at my shirt and it wasn't as soiled as before and my ribs didn't hurt as much. I took one last look at everything before picking up the burner cell phone to place two important calls. The sound of the ringing phone in my ear sent an eerie feeling through my body, as I knew I was playing with fire. I hadn't dialed this number in years. The last time we spoke I wasn't this desperate and they were new on the force.

"Compton police department, detective Henderson." The husky voice yelled.

"It's been a while." I said.

The line went silent but I could hear the detective breathing and shuffling around in his seat.

"Is this a good number?" the detective asked.

"Yes!" I replied.

The detective hung up. I sat thinking if my freedom was coming to an end. Did my plea of desperation create my own destiny to orange jumpers and prison food? The loud knock at the door snapped me out of my nightmare thoughts.

"Yeah!" I yelled.

Townsend opened the door and asked if I was ready to carve out the heart of the person who put me in this position. I looked at him thinking to myself it would be hard to do that type of bodily harm to myself. The prepaid gadget interrupted our criminal discussion. Townsend told me to take the call and closed the door. My heart began racing as I picked up the cell phone to answer. I stood up and walked out of the bedroom to the front door. I looked out of the front window to see if there was a team of black and whites with their department issued drawn and telling me to come up with my hands up. My paranoia subsided when I saw no one but law abiding citizens walking their dog of choice and sitting on their porches enjoying their freedom. My freedom was on a limited loan and the trustees were looking 24/7 for my ass.

I finally answered the cell phone.

"Henderson?"

"Am I talking to a ghost? Where the hell are you?" he asked.

"That's not important. I need some help." I said.

"Shit! You need more than help. The search has been turned over to the FBI." He yelled.

"Can you help me or not? Who's looking for me is the least of my concern." I told him.

"What could I possibly help you with Lance?"

Why in the hell did he say my name?

"Do you still know someone in the Transportation Security Agency?" I asked him.

"Are you thinking about leaving the country? Not a bad idea." He said laughingly.

My patience had already grown thin with the childish banter but I needed his help. I was at his mercy. I had no way of finding Maison without some assistance. Henderson abruptly told me to meet him at 7 PM at the old tire shop on Rosecrans just before the 710 freeway. Then he hung up. I sat there thinking about the desperation I must have conveyed but also wondered if I was walking into a trap. Henderson could be looking for that big promotion and turning me in would be just the lottery ticket to a top city official position. I turned on the television and the news enhanced my paranoia.

Reporting live from LAX, I'm Amanda Tgyuen and we are awaiting the arrival of Los Angeles police office Thaddeus Flame who was arrested in Florida for kidnapping and facing 2 felony counts. Officer Flame claims he is innocent. His first arraignment will be in 2 weeks. Back to you Aaron in the studio.

I told Townsend I needed the keys to his car to make a run. My first time behind the wheel of a car since I'd been shot and a first chance to see if I could go unnoticed in the streets. Townsend gave me an angry look and asked if I was up for that challenge or did he need to come along? Before I could respond he asked where was I going and who was I going to meet? I stood there like a teenager kid asking his parent for the keys to their car. I knew he could handle his own, but I needed to test my strength and get reacquainted with the outside world. I just stuck my hand out for the keys. He tossed the keys to me; told me to be careful and to call if I couldn't handle things myself. I turned and walked away without saying anything. When I walked out onto the porch, the nurse was pulling up. We exchanged dirty looks but no words were spoken. As I sat down in the front seat the pain in my ribs returned to get my attention. I started the Crown Victoria and proceeded to either my last place of freedom or someone who would lend me all the help I needed. As I backed out of the driveway I looked in the rearview mirror and the reflection I saw revealed anger, pain, and ridicule. Chasing love had cost me everything and had me on the run for my life. As much as I wanted to blame Maison and Kennedy, the real culprit of my condition was resting easy at an assisted living facility in Charlotte, North Carolina. Why couldn't she stand up for us to that trifling piece of shit of a man? Her love for him left none for me and I had to fend for myself. What the streets taught me definitely wasn't love. It was survival of the fittest and each of my wounds came from a lesson I learned the hard way.

Driving to the meeting place thoughts of Catalina came into my frontal. Townsend hadn't mentioned her since he rescued me and it was clear he didn't want to hear about her anymore. As I approached the traffic light I saw two police cars across the intersection from me. I pulled the bib of my cap down and made sure I followed the traffic laws. I cautiously made the right turn and applied the gas pedal smoothly so that I didn't accelerate too fast. I kept my eyes on the two police cars behind me through the side view mirror as I drove under the posted speed limit of 45 MPH.

When I turned on Rosecrans Avenue I felt uneasy and free at the same time. I hadn't had any contact with the outside world in quite a while. I let the window down and inhaled as much polluted air as I could and let my ears enjoy the sounds of road raging horns blowing and unruly drivers cursing at one another. When I first moved to the bear flag state this part of town was run down and infested with gang activity. Slowly the Latinos took over and every other store was no longer black owned but still many black buyers. The great city of Compton had improved with the vision of the newly elected black female mayor. Once a city to avoid and a freeway exit to pass, the city was known for circulating generations of African American dollars. Slowly, the mentality was changing and the crime was dropping. There's still a few lurking in the dark; one of them Detective Henderson. Before meeting him I felt the urge to stop inside one of the local coffee shops. I turned into a parking lot off of Rosecrans and slowly surveyed it for the men in blue. The busy shopping center wasn't thinking about me, I was the paranoid one. I stepped out of the car and adjusted my ball cap before entering the coffee shop. The walls of the narrow space had fancy art on the walls. The ritzy chocolate brown sofas were filled with daily brew drinkers and WIFI clientele. In front of the counter were appetizing baked goods for your selection. The line was long but moving briskly. I didn't know the last hour my face had graced the local news so I kept my head down as the line progressed. When I reached the counter, a young vibrant barista greeted me.

"Welcome to Lulu's, what's your blend of choice today?" She asked

"Yes! Do you serve cafe con leche?" I asked.

"Yes sir we do. What size?" She inquired.

"Medium, please." I replied.

"One medium cafe con leche; your total is $7.69." she said.

I reached into my pocket and pulled out one of the crisp $100 bills and handed it to the chipper young lady behind the counter. Without any hesitation she pulled out a counterfeit marker to authenticate the currency. Then the register opened and she counted back my change. Towards the end of her counting she asked a question that had many implications?

"You look familiar, are you a regular?" she queried.

Do I answer or leave immediately without my medium Spanish brew? The young barista continued the inquiry with "*I know I know your face.*"

"I get that a lot. No I'm not a regular to answer your

question." I replied.

As I move down the counter to wait for my order, I could see the puzzled look on her face as she helped the next customer. Lucky for me there were no televisions inside the cozy den of latte drinkers and alkaline water lovers. I remained calm waiting for my order to be called then it happened. The vibrant minimum wage worker must have recalled where she saw my face because she started moving frantically and shaking her head nonstop. She called another worker over to take over her register and I saw her pull out one of the latest smart phones. I leaned over the counter and asked how much longer on the medium con leche. My inquiry was ignored as the staff continued making a variety of gourmet roasted bean drinks. When I looked at the national inquirer again our eyes locked. She looked at her phone quickly then back at me then back to her phone. She covered her mouth and her eyes grew as wide as two football fields as she moved slowly down to my end of the counter. She didn't say a word but kept moving slowly behind the busy caffeine workstation. Damn I wanted my cafe con leche but I too had started to move slowly away from the waiting area. She didn't draw attention to her movement. The area was crowded and I couldn't run directly to the door without knocking over someone's dark or light roasted delight. The eavesdropping cashier bumped into one of her coworkers not stopping her undeviating pace with all eyes on me. I was a few feet away from the pick up counter when I heard *medium cafe con leche.* I looked at the door to exit then at the acne afflicted young boy holding my Spanish craving. The eyewitness was looking over one of the coffee machines at me now, not moving but focused. I moved towards the pick up counter to claim my craving watching her the entire time. When I got closer to the counter I saw her raise her smart phone to her right ear. Shit! I knew for sure my cover had been blown and the ball cap didn't work. I grabbed my medium blend and rushed for the door. Just as I exited I saw her still on the phone pointing in my direction. I sprinted to my car spilling some of my hot craving on my hand. Adrenaline at its highest I didn't even feel the hot liquid. It's not like I could sue them yet alone return for a refill. Once I made it to my car I looked back in the direction of the door, no sign of the eyewitness and I didn't hear any sirens. I started the car and pulled back onto Rosecrans Avenue headed to meet Henderson. I didn't speed but drove a little over the speed limit. My eyes looked in the rear view mirror every few seconds and scanned oncoming traffic. The traffic light at Rosecrans

Avenue and Santa Fe Avenue turn red as I approached the intersection. Directly across the intersection was a black and white cruiser with blue and red lights with two officers inside. There was a car in the lane next to me so I couldn't turn right on Santa Fe Avenue without someone doing a car insurance jingle. I sat tapping the steering wheel with one foot on the brake and the other *over* the gas pedal to floor it if need be. I saw the blue and red lights flash bright, then the siren blasted aloud. My foot was over the gas pedal but I didn't release my other foot from the brake. The police cruiser sped through the intersection but not towards me. A few seconds later the traffic light turned green and I proceeded on to meet Detective Henderson. I did not speed but I wasn't a Sunday driver either. As I drove towards the tire shop I saw two sets of flashing blue and red lights coming in my direction. I crossed Long Beach Boulevard and passed by an old well-known park affiliated with one of Compton's meanest gangs on the right. I could see the lights getting closer through the rear view mirror. The inquisitive barista must have seen my vehicle pull away. I started looking for a side street to turn down very quickly. I needed this meeting with Henderson to happen. I couldn't lead the men in black right to me. They'd have to work a little harder than that. I still had a few blocks to go as I approached Atlantic Avenue. Just ahead of me I saw two more police cruiser rolling fast towards me with no siren and no flashing blue and red lights. My vehicle information had gone viral on the police scanner. I pulled my weapon from under the seat and slid it under my right leg. The silent cruisers were approaching from the opposite flow of traffic. I maintained my current speed getting closer to Atlantic Avenue. A few seconds went by before the silent cruisers swerved quickly towards my direction, the sirens blasting now and my getaway options extremely limited. I floored the gas pedal as one of the cruisers slammed into the back corner spinning me slightly. My killer instinct returned instantly and I pulled the weapon from under my leg and began unloading bullets towards the police cruisers. Traffic on the busy street came to a stop and many had pulled out their smart phones to capture the local action. Compton's finest not knowing I was en route to meet one of their respected detectives returned fire shattering the back glass and piercing holes in the side of my freedom chariot. My gun was out of ammunition and I needed to reload to continue this copper filled conversation. I sped away as I heard gunfire in my direction. Once I passed Atlantic Avenue I made a hard left hand turn on Williams Avenue and sped through the quiet neighborhood of Spanish stucco homes towards McMillian street. I parked quickly and ran up a narrow driveway. In the back yard there were some Latino men drinking and playing dominoes. They immediately noticed me and asked me if I knew where I was as they approached. I made a mad dash for the cement wall and hopped over it into another yard where a German shepherd met me. He raised his head but didn't bother running after me. I could hear the sirens close by but I kept moving quickly to get to the tire shop to meet Henderson. I jumped over another cement wall and walked normal towards the meeting spot. I could see it at the end of the block and I could also hear the sirens coming closer. There was a block separating me from either meeting with Henderson or going back into police custody.

When I walked through the open bay I saw Henderson standing by the front office door with a medium size cup in his hand talking to one of the mechanics. He spotted me and showed an evil smile. I moved through the bay of cars getting new treads or some unexpected repair from the diagnostic check. When I walked up to Henderson he said 'you sure know how to make an entrance'. Just then a black and white pulled up.

"Detective Henderson! Have you seen a black male, medium build wearing a baseball cap?" yelled the driver.

I was knelt down behind a large tool cabinet on wheels. My heart was beating fast and I felt like it was going to pop right out of my body. I hadn't spoken to Henderson in over a year so I wasn't really sure if he would turn me in or keep his hands grimy. What felt like an eternity was really seconds before I heard his response.

"No! I haven't seen anyone." He said.

The driver of the black and white asked him to keep a look out for anyone fitting the description and respond with any force necessary. Then he sped off. I looked up at Henderson and asked if the coast was clear. He took a sip from his medium size cup never making eye contact with me and said nonchalantly "yep".

"Thanks." I told him.

"You've got yourself in one of heck of a mess." He said.

"I'm sure you've stepped on a few landmines." I replied.

"So what can I do for a wanted man?" He arrogantly asked.

"It may cost you your badge. You up for that?" I inquired.

"My badge is on the line every day I wake up." He said.

"You took a legal oath. This involves the other side of the law." I informed.

"That's funny. Get to it before another black and white rolls through and I change my mind." He yelled.

"I need you to go to my home and get a few things." I told him.

His left eyebrow squinted and his eyes got smaller. His mind was trying to figure out what I was up. He took another sip from his cup, sat it down on the tool cabinet and looked out into the flow of traffic on Rosecrans Avenue. Then he reached inside the left side of his blazer and pulled out his department issued; walked towards me and grabbed my shirt with his gun under my chin and told me if I screwed him over he would see to it that I lived the rest of my natural life in pain until he felt like killing me. Mentally I didn't hear anything he said. I wanted one answer yes or no. Our eyes remained locked, no words only the noise from the tire shop. Henderson finally lowered his gun and released my shirt. After he holstered his weapon he picked his medium size cup up and said in a low voice – "when do we get started?"

"I need one other thing." I said.

"You have enough to cover it?" he asked.

"I'm good for it." I said.

"What is it?" he snarled.

"I need to know everything going on with the cop that was arrested in Florida." I said.

"Damn! Who haven't you used Lance." He asked.

"The state should pay their law enforcement more. He came to me if you must know." I told him.

"You're right about the pay." He laughed.

Henderson walked out unto Rosecrans Avenue to see if his colleagues were still in the area. The loud sirens were gone and the helicopter was no longer circling above. I walked to the edge of the bay but not far enough to be seen. Henderson got into his unmarked vehicle and motioned for me to come to him. He asked me if I needed a ride someplace before he left. I told him I left my car back on McMillian Street but I wasn't sure if his colleagues had figured that out. He grinned and said it's probably still there before starting his car. I got in on the passenger side and we pulled off. Something didn't feel right. Even with the gun tactic, Henderson took my offer too easy with very little investigation. I'm sure he had made a few illegal scores while being on the police force. Maybe his soul was empty like mine and never found the true meaning of life. When we pulled off the rogue police officer began his inquiry.

"So what do you need from your home and where is it?" he asked.

"I need some equipment to do what I do best and I have a small amount of cash." I told him.

"You planning on taking out the whole police department?" he asked.

"No! Just two individuals and whoever stands in my way." I said.

"Not my concern. When would you like for me to go?" He asked.

"Can we meet tomorrow and head up there?" I asked.

"If you're going, you don't need me." He said.

"You might forget the equipment and just grab the small stash and vanish. It's not like I can file a police report." I said.

We pulled up to my car and I told Henderson to meet me at the Chevron gas station on Vermont St and Los Feliz Blvd, then we'd go from there. He took another sip from his cup and nodded. I got out of the car and he sped off with no hesitation. I walked towards my abandoned vehicle to head back to Townsends when my cell phone rang. I looked at the screen. It was the rogue detective. Had he changed his mind? I didn't answer because that's what he wanted me to do. He wanted me to feel desperate. He wanted to feel needed. But truthfully I didn't need him. One way or another I was going to get my equipment and the small stash. Unfortunately, the police departments were full of underpaid underappreciated workers looking to make an extra buck or two. I had no problem using them as pawns to get what I wanted. Henderson called two more times but didn't leave a message. If it was that important he could have said it before he pulled off in such a hurry.

I called Townsend and told him I was headed back to his place and that we needed to make a few stops. Like Townsend, when I was finished saying everything, he didn't say anything he just disconnected the call. I looked at the phone and tried to remember the young lady's name that worked in the print shop chasing Hollywood stardom. I couldn't recall anything but her area code of 562. Traffic was heavy but moving steady. I didn't speed or make any traffic violations to call attention to myself. I'm sure the police were still listening intently to their scanners for any possible sightings of me.

I turned onto the street in Compton where I was hiding out and healing. I approached the house and I saw two police cars in front. Two officers had Townsend on the porch questioning him. Their backs were turned to the street so they didn't see me drive past. Townsend was able to give me the nod to let me know he had everything under control. I drove past the house without the police catching a view of me. When I made it to the end of the block I made a right turn and headed to Athens Park to wait for Townsend's phone call.

Sitting at the park thoughts of my childhood and Maxine Boatwright flooded my mind. I had so many unanswered questions for her. Unfortunately her health state barely allowed her to remember her own name, what day of the week it was and normal things a person should know. As I sat there I saw kids playing with each other. I saw adult males playing catch with younger boys and maybe it wasn't their father; perhaps an uncle, a cousin or an older brother but at least it was a male figure. I jogged my memory and couldn't recall a male figure in my life. My father was too busy drinking then eventually doing drugs. Before his life ended he was stealing from us, sleeping in my mother's bed giving her God knows what diseases he caught from the filthy streets and crack houses he frequented. Maxine didn't make things better because she held on to his hallowed word of returning and making it better for them. It was always about "them"; my well-being was barely a conversation. Even my school clothes and shoes were from the local Goodwill stores. I hated the first day of school because all of the other kids had bright new clothes and clean shoes with no holes or rips. My clothes were dull with mismatched buttons and loose pockets on the pants. Most times my shoe soles were close to bare. My shirts were dingy. Winters were the worst because the long sleeved shirts were short on my arms and I never had a winter coat; at best a sweatshirt with a hood and no gloves. But before my father's habits changed he and Maxine were always in new threads and stayed well fed. I remember one Easter in particular. I was 14 and Maxine had cooked a roast, twice baked potatoes, fresh greens and a peach cobbler. As we sat at the table, while my mother was making my plate I heard my father ask her in an angry voice if I was going to eat all of that food she was putting on my plate. I slumped my shoulders and didn't even touch the roast. I just ate the potatoes and green beans. I didn't ask for dessert but later that night Maxine came to my room with a small plate of warm roast beef and some cobbler. She was so nervous that it made me uncomfortable. But in her softest voice she told me to eat up and have sweet dreams. That night I don't know what gave me the strength but I asked Maxine if the man living with us was my real father? She rubbed my shoulders gently and softly said of course he is Lance. I continued asking her why he never did anything with me. Why he never registered me for sports. Why he never threw a ball with me; any kind of ball. Why didn't he talk to me about girls or teach me how to fight. The man she said was my real father never taught me the things I saw other little boys learning from the adult males in their lives. I learned to ride a bike on my own. I believe I sprained my shoulder learning how to throw a football and playing catch with myself while he was hanging with his friends. When I played with the other kids I could see the difference in their skills versus mine; a lot for any kid to stomach on a daily basis. I would see them on the weekends wearing the seasonal sports jersey from the park and recreation center and eventually trophies from the end of the season banquet. I didn't have trophies and medals hanging from my shelves, just ugly school pictures with Goodwill clothes. Maybe a decent hair cut if the man living there had time to take me to the barber. Before my mother left my room she told me don't mind my father and that he loves me. That was easy for her say. I never saw her sneaking to eat the rest of her dinner or wearing raggedy clothes and torn shoes. I heard him tell her he loved her every time he left the house but he never told me he loved me. Before I fell asleep that night, I told myself I had to get out of that house as soon as possible. Joining the Army was my ticket out of an unloved and unwanted house. Unlike the other soldiers writing home, I never wrote letters. I would call Maxine every other weekend to see how she was doing. I never asked about my father and apparently he never asked about me because she would never tell me 'your father said hello Lance'.

My miserable existence of a childhood memory was rescued by the irritating ringing of the cell phone resting on my leg. It was Townsend.

"What did the police want?" I nervously asked.

"They were responding to an anonymous tip." He said.

"Me?" I inquired.

"Yes! How they found out I have no idea but I brought everything important with me. We can't go back there." He snarled.

"Did you get……"

"I have your stuff! No time for stupid questions Lance." He yelled.

"So what's your plan Lance? We don't have many more places to hide." He said.

"I met with an old detective buddy and he's going to get some things from my house. Then I can put everything in motion." I said.

Townsend didn't respond instead he asked where was I

so we could get off of the streets for the evening. I told him I was parked at Athens Park on the 124th Street side. He sharply said ok and the phone went dead. I sat back and started to think about who I was going to kill first, which one was going to suffer the longest and the most. The thoughts of smelling blood and torturing someone's body awakened the spirits inside of me. The damage I plan to do would make it hard for dental records to even identify the remains. When Townsend pulled up, my car was running and in reverse ready to move. He didn't like small talk and my old self was returning – neither did I.

I followed Townsend up El Segundo Boulevard heading west towards Western Ave. From Western Ave we turned on 122nd Street and parked at a house between Denker Avenue and Normandie Avenue. There were two houses on the lot. One towards the front of the street and the other sat back about 30 yards or so. Townsend told me to pull up in the driveway and park behind the first house. There was a light on inside the first house but the second house was completely dark. We entered through a side door that had black bars on the door; not uncommon in this part of Los Angeles. The first room we walked through looked like a washing room. I didn't see any clothes laying around and the washer and dryer looked barely used. The next room was the kitchen that had stainless steel appliances and tile flooring. Off to the right I saw the dining room. Then my open house tour ended when I saw the rude nurse who treated my wounds in Compton. Her attitude remained consistent as she walked past me and rolled her eyes before hugging Townsend and telling him everything was in place. She left the room just as quickly as she had entered it. Townsend motioned for me to follow him. It was a small walk through the dining room down a hall that opened up into a decent size room. Inside the room were two computers, police scanners, a table with cell phones and an open cabinet displaying automatic weapons. I counted fifteen weapons hanging inside the closet and twenty boxes of ammunition stacked at the bottom of the cabinet. My eyes lit up like a child inside a toy store. I saw four HK416s, a couple of M4s, six CZ 75 SP-01 9mm and two Mossberg pump rifles. I approached the cabinet and lifted one of the M4s. My strength was strong enough to hold it but I wasn't sure I could handle pulling the trigger. I positioned the weapon in my left hand and in the crevice of my right shoulder and aimed it at one of the walls. I closed my right eye and aligned my sights pretending Maison was in front of me and squeezed the trigger.

"Are you ready to add to your body count?" Townsend

asked.

I kept the rifle pointed at the wall then said,

"Yes!"

"Are you going to kill that young rookie cop Lance?" he asked.

"Are you getting emotional on me?" I replied.

"Not at all! Just didn't know he was an issue."

"Anyone who wants me dead is an issue." I told him.

I lowered the weapon and returned it to the cabinet. I walked over to the table and picked up one of the cell phones and asked Townsend if they were international capable. He nodded yes. I pulled out the manila envelope Little Red gave me. I pulled out the information where Maison was vacationing. He had flown off to Mermerli beach in Antalya Turkey. I sat down and started to dial the international number. Townsend sat next to me and powered up the computers and turned on the scanners. I heard the international call ringing very low with a lot of clicking. Was Little Red full of crap or had he come through better than a AAA travel agent. As the phone rang, a feeling of repugnance got my stomach's attention. My mind went back to the ambush and visions of Catalina standing there because of me. I clenched my fist and my jaw got tight. After six rings I heard a soft voice answer.

She said Merhaba three or four times before I said hello.

"lyi gunler, ben Dilek Aspen Antalya oteli aradiginiz icin tesekkur ederiz. Nasil yardicmi olabilirim?"

"Chambers beyin odasini baglarmisiniz lutfen." I said

"Memnuniyetle, bir saniye efendim, baglayim." She replied.

The phone rang twice before I heard his ghastly voice answer. It was a few minutes after 6 AM local time for him.

"What is it?" he yelled.

"Is that how you greet an old friend?" I asked.

I heard him rustling around. He cleared his throat and I heard him tell someone to move.

"Listen, whoever this is, stop wasting my time." He said.

"Trust me, you wasted enough time for both of us." I said.

"Who is this?" he yelled again.

"The last person you'll see before you join your nosey daughter!" I snarled.

The phone was silent for a few seconds.

"Lance? I left you dying by the side of your immigrant housekeeper." He said laughing.

"You should've made sure I took my last breath. That's what happens when a boy tries to do a man's job. I won't make the same mistake." I told him.

"How did you find me?" he asked.

"That's not important. You should be concerned about your life and your family in Omaha." I told him.

"Omaha? How did you….

I cut him off.

"Don't waste your time Maison. I could make one phone call and you'd never see or hear from them again." I said.

"You're bluffing." He laughed.

"Laugh now because you're a dead man. I won't rest until your corpse is cut up into so many pieces that the coroner will donate your body to research instead of doing an autopsy." I told him.

"I see you're still issuing juvenile threats." He said.

"That's a promise my friend." I said.

"We're not friends!" he said jokingly.

"You're right and I must be going now. I have a plane to catch." I told him.

He didn't respond but I could hear noise in the background of his room. Someone was knocking at his room door.

"See you soon Maison. You should answer your door." I hung up.

I turned and joined Townsend in front of the computer screens and emptied the manila folder with Maison's information. While he's enjoying the Mediterranean his life is about to come crashing down. First I loaded all of his bank account information into an encrypted database. That database will hack into all of his accounts and start making transfers of small amounts into an untraceable account similar to the bit coin. By the time Maison notices, a sizable amount will already be gone and his life will be nonexistent. Next I located all of his personal as well as his business real estate. If he thought losing his daughter was hard, wait until he sees what I have in store for his family in Omaha and for him. His death will be an unsolved mystery for years to come. I looked at Townsend and told him I needed him to get a city truck, a city electric uniform and post up on Los Feliz Blvd not too far from Vermont tomorrow night. I wanted him in place in case Henderson decided he would keep everything he got from my house. Without hesitation, Townsend nodded and told me he'd be there ready. I know he didn't want to hear my next request but I told him I needed him to locate Catalina. His look of disgust told me how he felt without room for misinterpretation. I ignored his facial expression and restated the request with more emphasis of importance. He got up and walked outside. I opened up the Internet browser on one of the computers and typed in the web address for my cell phone carrier. I typed in my user name and what I thought was my password but I was unsuccessful. I tried once again but no luck getting into my account. I clicked on the link to reset my password and another screen appeared asking me to answer my security questions. Oh boy I'm not sure I remember the answers to those questions either. After two attempts I was able to get the right answers and the reset your password screen appeared. I had to find Sydney's number so hopefully I hadn't dialed too many 562 area code numbers. I looked at my phone bills starting from 4 months prior. A couple of numbers were dialed repeatedly and I had texted those same numbers – Maison and Thad. I kept searching through my bill until I found a 562 area code number. There was one I had called at 9:32 AM and followed up with a text a few minutes later. I picked up one of the untraceable cell phones and dialed the 562 area code number. The number began ringing and believe it or not I wasn't exactly sure what I would ask Sydney. I wasn't even sure she would talk to me, as I'm certain she'd seen all of the news about my unlawful lifestyle. It was much different than the one I had portrayed to her. The voice that answered sounded as if they were in a deep sleep. They said hello.

"May I speak to Sydney?" I asked sheepishly.

"Sydney?" The voice asked irritated.

"Yes is this Sydney?" I asked.

"No! Who is this?" The voice yelled.

"I'm an old friend. I must've dialed the wrong number." I said.

"At this hour people don't dial the wrong number". She said.

"I apologize. Have a good evening." I pleaded before hanging up.

After I hung up I went back to the computer and continued looking at more old phone numbers on my bill. I was rudely interrupted when the cell phone I just used rang out loud. These phones according to Townsend were brand new burner phones with untraceable SIM cards. There was no number displayed on the small screen. I looked at the phone but didn't answer it. I continued my search for Sydney's number. I came across another telephone number with a 562 area code but before I could dial it, the same cell phone started ringing. I was annoyed. Who could be calling this brand new cell phone? I looked at the phone and felt compelled to answer it; anxious to hear the voice on the other end. Who had tracked me down?

"You couldn't let sleeping dogs lie?" the voice said.

I didn't recognize the voice. It wasn't Henderson. It wasn't my old friend Eduardo. I was drawing a blank.

"Who is this?" I asked timidly.

"Oh come on. You killed her brother and then have the nerve to call her. You truly are a piece of work." The voice said.

Oh my God, the 562 area code number was Jordan. Who was this calling me seconds later after I hung up?

"So what are you? Her voice of reasoning?" I asked.

"No I'm your sacrificial lamb that survived the slaughter." The voice said.

How had he found me before I found him? It was Thad. I stood up and looked around the room. My trust meter sprang to the lowest level with Townsend immediately. It had to be him because I hadn't called Henderson from this cell phone.

"Are you there Lance?" Thad asked.

"Yes! No need for the unnecessary banter. Who will stop breathing first is the only question?" I said.

"My money is on you!" He said.

"I see you don't mind losing again." I said.

"I was at an unfair advantage last time." Thad said.

"And you think you're in a better position this time.

Aren't you facing felony kidnapping charges?" I asked.

Thad laugh loudly before replying.

"Lance, you're on every law enforcement agency's radar. You can only hide for so long." He said.

"Stay safe Thad." I said and hung up.

When I turned around Townsend was standing there and he asked what was that about? I didn't answer him immediately. I just looked at him. Our bond went back long before I pulled the trigger on my first paid hit. He folded his arms across his chest; growing annoyed at my nonresponse.

"Where did you get these damn phones from?" I asked.

"First of all check your tone with me." He shouted.

"Answer the question Townsend." I shouted back.

"I'm not answering a damn thing." He said.

"So this is how our relationship is going to play out?" I asked.

"You're a man. Make your decision." He yelled.

"Someone traced the cell phone I just used." I said.

"Nonsense!" He yelled.

"The cop I'm after called me after I made one phone call." I said.

"What does that have to do with me?" He asked.

"You got the phones. So you tell me." I snarled.

"Did you call him?" He asked with attitude.

"Of course I did not call him!"

"Well whoever you called doesn't have nothing to do with me." He said and walked away.

"Townsend!" I yelled.

He walked out of the room and slammed the door. I kept calling his name until I started cursing him out to myself. One thing's for certain, I had dialed Jordan's number. Now she too had a cell phone number to reach me and turn over to the police. I hope I don't have to kill her as well. I threw the phone up against the wall and watched it crumble to the floor. I walked to the front of the house where Townsend was sitting in a recliner. He had lit up a cigar and was listening to some music. Before I could say anything he blurted out.

"Lance, I just want to relax. I don't have time for your foolishness." He said.

I charged the chair he was sitting in and both of us landed on the floor. I threw the first punch to his mouth. He swung his knee into my ribs. I fell to the floor and he crawled over to me and punched me in my left jaw. Then he punched me in my stomach twice. I managed to kick him back. When I stood up I yelled where did the phones come from? He said vulgar words then charged me throwing a punch to my jaw again. I staggered but was able to throw a punch back to his left eye. We exchanged blows to each other's body then to the face, both of us bleeding. The nurse came running in yelling and screaming for us to stop it. She was standing in between us. I was holding my ribs and I could feel the dampness through my shirt.

"Lance is washed up and paranoid. Let's get out of here." Townsend said.

"Whatever! The rookie cop didn't dial the number by luck. Now did he?" I snapped.

"You're crazy! I dropped everything I had going on in New York to come rescue you. The last thing I'd do is turn you in for some chump change reward money. Come at me again like that and I'll shoot you myself." He said.

"Yeah! Well maybe New York wasn't working out? Perhaps the chump change was enough to lure you out here. And why haven't you found Catalina yet?" I snarled.

"A damn immigrant housekeeper should be the last thing on your mind. You're wanted for murder, kidnapping and clearly have lost your damn mind. Don't ask me about Catalina again until you've at least killed Maison or the young cop." Townsend yelled at me.

Then he and the annoying nurse walked out of the front door.

Townsend was right. I had run a foul by accusing him of setting me up and physically attacking him. He was all I had out here in my pursuit of killing Maison and Thad. I dropped my head in shame and went back to the computer screens in search of Sydney's number. I picked up another cell phone and dialed the last 562 area code number I saw before the rogue cop interrupted me. Each time I heard the phone ring, an eerie feeling stirred inside me. After six rings the phone went to voicemail but there was no personal greeting. I hung up and kept scrolling through my bill. I found two more numbers with the area code I was in search for but both numbers were no longer in service. I turned the computers off and walked through the empty house to a bedroom that had a queen size bed, a nightstand and dresser. There was a bathroom connected to the bedroom. I looked inside the tiny closet in the hallway for towels. It wasn't too many things inside. There were three bath towels, one wash cloth, a couple of new toothbrushes, some bed linen and some assorted soaps. I reached for one of the bath towels, the washcloth and a bar of unscented soap. When I walked back into the bathroom I turned the shower on and stood looking in the mirror as the water warmed. Looking at the man in the mirror brought nothing but pain. I didn't see a wrinkle of hope or happiness. I wondered if I'd ever see Townsend again. Pride aside I knew I needed him to pull this off but I couldn't bring myself to beg anyone for anything. After I finished showering I laid in the empty house on the uncomfortable bed thinking would my life as I once knew it ever be the same? Would someone hire my services again? Would I ever find the one thing that would make me whole? If I did find it how would I handle it and how long would it be before I messed it up with my tormented demons, revenge seekers and multiple untouched landmines.

It was just before dawn when I woke up the next morning. The quietness was peaceful and scary. I was hoping to hear Townsend moving about in one of the rooms. I got up and walked through the house to only find it still empty. I looked out the front window and didn't see anything but the black sedan I drove the day prior. To hell with him then! I felt a slight pain in my ribs but I stretched before I did a home workout. I needed to test my strength for what lies ahead. After my workout I turned on the television and the same image of me as before was in the corner of the background as a male news reporter spoke.

The whereabouts of Lance Goodman is still unknown at this time. Police are searching for the suspect who is considered armed and very dangerous. If you see this man please call 911.

I flipped through the channels until I found a sports channel. Highly unlikely my face and search report would be on a channel like this. The sports ticker showed the latest scores of basketball, hockey and tennis championships as a commercial for men's hair shampoo played in the background. I turned the television off because I was annoyed already. I was mad at myself and I couldn't focus. But I needed to be because I was on my own with Henderson this evening. Once his eyes saw how much money was at my house he could test me and not give me a penny of it. I couldn't let that happen especially since Townsend has vanished. I got dressed and grabbed some of the hardware before I left the house. I needed a good cup of Joe and some breakfast. The last time I stopped for coffee it didn't go so well. I had to find someplace that wasn't so busy and the workers weren't so nosey. I started my only means of transportation and looked in the rear view mirror. I hated the image I saw. As I was backing out of the driveway I saw a black and white police car approaching from the left. I could see the two officers looking in my direction. The police squad car slowed a bit as it got closer to the house so I pulled one of the handguns out and chambered a round, then put it on the seat next to me. I was closer to the end of the driveway now and we made eye contact. It was a white officer and black officer. Both of them looked seasoned and not trigger happy. As they passed the driveway my eyes never left the car and my right hand was around the pistol grip and the safety was released ready for action if need be. The police cruiser reached the end of the block and stopped at the stop sign. I could see the brake lights blaring brightly as they remained in place. I kept the car in reverse but held my position in the driveway. Then the brake lights on the police cruiser went dim and I saw the squad car speed through the intersection and make a U-turn in my direction. I didn't make an attempt to run away. I just sat in the driveway with my foot still on the brake and my hand on the gun. As they got closer they turned on the siren and the flashing red and blue lights. Now I had to make a decision. Do I punch the gas pedal and ram into them instantly initiating a police chase, increasing my chances of going back into police custody or calmly handle the situation?

"Good morning Sir! You mind turning off the vehicle?" The black officer said.

I had slid the gun under my seat and the small duffle bag with the other weapons under the passenger seat.

"Sure officer. Is there something wrong?" I asked.

"Why were you still in the driveway? When we passed, you were backing out." He inquired.

"I was just finishing up a text message before I started driving." I told him.

I saw him looking through the vehicle with his right hand around his department issued firearm. Just then I saw in the rearview mirror another black and white cruiser pull up.

"Do you have some ID?" He asked.

"Yes I do." I replied.

"Let me see it and your vehicle registration." He demanded. His voice was stern.

I reached inside the glove compartment to get the registration, pulled out my ID from my front pocket and handed it to the officer.

"You don't have a wallet?" The officer asked.

"Haven't carried one since I was kid." I told him.

"Hang tight. I'll be right back." He said.

I watched the officer walk back to the squad car to run my new identity and vehicle information. It didn't take long for him to return with my fabricated identity. I saw the other squad car leave. He handed me back my credentials and told me to have a good day. As soon as they drove off I backed out of the driveway and headed to the city of Paramount. There was a nice 2 generations family owned soul food restaurant that served breakfast just off the 91 Freeway close to Alondra Boulevard. As I drove the speed limit on the 110 Freeway I got excited thinking what I'd do once Henderson made that trip for me. Thoughts of Catalina were still swimming around my head at warp speed. I needed to know that she was alive and how I could get her back with me. Without a doubt we'd never be able to return to Los Feliz Hills but wherever I was headed I wanted her with me. She had been more of a mother to me than Maxine ever had. Catalina was loyal to me from day one. There were many days I'm sure she had her own suspicions but never said a word. The only real challenge of our relationship came when I brought those ungrateful juveniles to my home. I never should have played myself for a fool with them. Although leaving them with a drug goon wasn't the best idea either, I should've left well enough alone. I checked the cell phone I received from Little Red. No text messages or missed phone calls from Townsend. I exited the 91 Freeway and parked on the street not too far from the restaurant. When I walked into the restaurant there were three couples eating in the homelike establishment. One of the male workers immediately greeted me.

"Dine in for one?" he asked.

"Yes, please." I told him.

"Our special this morning is two eggs any style, country fried potatoes and honey maple ham steak for $6.99. Can I start you with something to drink?" he asked.

"Coffee please! No cream." I said.

He walked to get my drink. I hadn't been to this place in a couple of years. Not much had changed. The walls were filled with autographed framed pictures of celebrities who had stopped by for a meal. Artificial plant décor throughout, the tables were covered with white tablecloths and the chairs were black. When the waiter returned with my coffee I told him I'd have the special, eggs sunny side up and a side of rye toast. Sitting there waiting for my morning meal I couldn't help but observe the couples eating. Two were definitely in love and it pissed me off. What the hell was so special about love? Looking at one of the couples gazing into each other's eyes and smiling made my blood boil. The guy was playing with her right ear and she'd shy away and tap his hands. Then he grabbed her right hand and rubbed it never leaving her eyes. I seen her pick up one of the forks and feed him. I clenched my fists so tight my knuckles ached. I hadn't experienced that kind of affection in my life. The waiter returned with my plate of food and I didn't even thank him. My eyes still stuck on the lovebirds. The other couple was sitting next to each other holding hands, raising them often kissing the back of the other's hand. Such foolishness. They were laughing amongst themselves, probably about some silly moment going on between them. They had finished their meal and were having a small Danish cake. The guy was feeding her and playing with the utensil in her face. I shook my head and slammed the fork into my sunny side eggs. I'm sure they heard the fork against the plate. I didn't care. Their love sessions needed a damn break. Maybe they'd get smart and cut that shit out. The last couple was on their smart phones and not talking to each other. I imagine the love had set sail some time ago but neither one wanted to leave their comfort zones. They wandered through the day pretending it would get better. She hoping he'd change, he hoping she'd just leave making it easier. All the while the only thing changing was the time as it ticked away in their toxic relationship. No one wanted to take ownership of how they got to nonverbal communications sitting across from each other talking to everyone else but to one another. I slammed my fork against the plate for another bite of my eggs. My meal was the only thing bringing me satisfaction at this early hour. One of the couples stood up to leave holding hands and giving each other kisses. Good luck and good riddance. One disgusting couple left. Hopefully they were leaving soon so I could read the newspaper and enjoy the real world around me. People with real problems not this sappy love scene I just digested. The waiter returned and asked me if I needed anything else. Under my breath I told him to tell the interlock twosome to get a room and get the hell out of here.

"Some more coffee please." I told him.

"I'll bring you a fresh cup as well." He said.

The service was great but the environment was revolting. The headlines were about a prison break, two killed and three still at large. Some news about the political race, boycotting one of the award shows and whether Los Angeles is getting an NFL team again. I quickly flipped to the classified section to see if there was any work for me. You'd be surprised how the wording of hiring a hit man is legally printed in the local newspaper. I browsed but didn't see anything. I took two sips of my coffee. It was nice and hot. I pulled out my cell phone and returned Henderson's call. Had he reconsidered or had he put his own plan in effect to capture me. The phone rang three times before he answered.

"What took so long to call?" He asked with an attitude.

"Busy! What's up Henderson?" I asked annoyed.

"Are we still on for today?" He asked.

"Does L.A. have smog?" I asked.

"Even with your odds, you're still a smart ass!" he said.

"Anything else Henderson?" I asked.

"I suppose not." He replied.

"See you at 7! You know the location." I said and hung up.

After I hung up I dialed the unanswered number 562 number from last night again. The phone rang twice and then I heard her voice, that same innocent voice that walked in late from an audition. Hearing her say hello stunned me. I wasn't ready. I wasn't ready to have the conversation but I had a great acting opportunity for her. I finally spoke to my former employee.

"Hi Sydney!" I said.

"Hi! Who is this?" She asked.

I looked around the restaurant. Just the smartphone couple was there. I whispered as best I could.

"It's Lance." I said.

"Lance who?" She asked.

"Lance your old boss." I whispered.

The phone fell silent. What was she thinking? Was someone with her? Was she trying to get their attention? Was she about to hang up, write the number down and call the authorities? I needed her to say something. Whether she hung up and cursed me out, I needed closure or her forgiveness and willingness to help me.

"Lance! Oh my God! Are you okay? Are those things true what they're saying?" she asked.

I could hear her heart racing through the phone.

"Sydney! Calm down, can we meet?" I asked.

"Meet where? The news says you're armed and dangerous. I don't know Lance." She said.

She said 'I don't know'. That meant she still had some faith in me but questioned herself about how involved should she get with me.

"Sydney, I promise to explain everything to you face to face but not over the phone." I told her.

I could hear her heavy breathing.

"Lance! I don't, I don't….know about this." She said.

"I know you have a lot of questions. I really need to meet with you. Please Sydney." I begged.

She didn't respond but I could hear her fidgeting. Something evil stirred inside of me and I became annoyed with her indecisiveness. After all of the times I turned my head to her auditions and tardy arrivals. Okay superstar, have it your way. I don't beg anyone for a damn thing.

"Sydney!" I said.

"Yes Lance, what is it?" she shouted.

"Take care!" I said and hung up.

This meeting was going to either make or break me; a sure test of Henderson's crooked character. I asked the helpful waiter if I could get my coffee in a to go cup. He returned with a medium sized cup filled with hot coffee and placed packets of sugar, sweeteners, cream and a wooden stir stick on the table. He flashed his customer service smile and bid me a good day. I added some cream and one packet of sugar to the hot java and headed to the front to pay my check. As I approached the counter I felt the cell phone in my pocket vibrating. When I pulled it out and looked at the screen I didn't recognize the number so I ignored the call. I had no time to entertain telemarketers and misdials. By the time I paid my bill and got to the car, my cell phone was buzzing again from the same number. I pressed the talk button and answered in an annoyed tone.

"I can't believe I used to look up to you." The voice said.

"I've never considered myself anyone's hero. Who is this?" I asked.

"You're doing a lot of back tracking Lance. I never would've thought you of all people would beg and plead." The voice said.

Now I was annoyed beyond reason and knew who this was.

"Listen Thad, you're going to grow tired of tracking who I'm calling. I may be a wanted man but you're a dead man on borrowed time. You really should enjoy what time you have left on this earth." I said.

"Every cop on the streets is looking for you but not every cop is going to arrest you. Certain ones are going to bring you to me." He said.

"Oh yeah? You still call that studio off of Washington Boulevard home? You can barely walk around in there. Surely you couldn't do any damage there. You still in rookie mode." I said.

Thad found my comment humorous, then he responded.

"Seems to me you're the rookie. Enjoy your freedom while you can. It won't be much longer." He said.

The phone line went dead. Thad must be getting some help because I remember him being young and gullible. I'm still not worried at this point. As long as my meeting with Henderson goes as planned, both Maison and Thad will soon be memories to their loved ones and blessings to my empty soul. I pulled out into traffic and headed back towards the 91 Freeway enroute to Los Feliz Hills. Traffic was a little heavy but moving. I turned on the radio and tuned into the FM station that played a variety of jazz and R&B oldies. The current song playing was an oldie but goodie by the group WAR – *why can't we be friends*. By the time I reached the 110 Freeway I was in harmony with Lionel Richie blasting *Easy* as my anxiety levels increased and so did my speed and it was Sunday morning and I couldn't stand the pain. I saw a motorcycle cop a few cars ahead of me so slowed my speed. That was the music back then, strong lyrics with strong meaning. I tried more than enough times with the current artist in the music industry and just couldn't get into it. This young kid out of Compton did catch my ear but I can't remember the last time I downloaded a new song or album for that matter.

It was about 6:30 PM by the time I reached my old neighborhood. I was definitely taking a huge risk because I was a pillar of the community at one point and I'm sure if someone saw me they'd recognize my face. Traffic was a little heavy as I approached Vermont Avenue. Something must have been going on up the hill where I used to meet someone I thought was a friend. There were traffic policemen and women directing traffic at the intersection of Vermont Avenue and Los Feliz Boulevard. As I approached to make my left hand turn one of the female traffic cops motioned for me to stop then allowed the flow of traffic from across the intersection to proceed. She kept her whistle in her mouth and her eyes on me as she waved oncoming traffic. As I sat there waiting for *mother may I* to allow me to turn I thought about Catalina and her well-being. I hoped and wished so badly that she was still alive and that I would get a chance to make up for all of my wrongdoing. A loud whistle and a rapidly moving hand directing me to turn left interrupted my thoughts. I proceeded through the intersection down the street before making a U-turn to make my way back to the gas station on the corner. I turned in and parked by the air pump and restrooms. The same smooth radio station was playing more oldies but goodies. Sade was asking if it was a crime as I watched the flow of traffic and the traffic cops continue to direct traffic. There were three cars at the gas station that could sink me further. There was a lady sitting in one of the cars but wasn't pumping any of the war driven substance into her black two door coupe. I saw her hands frantically moving around inside and she appeared to be talking to someone through her vehicle's Bluetooth connection. I sat back and continued listening to Sade convince herself she still wanted someone and wanted them to still want her. The woman got out of her car and started walking around her vehicle looking for something. A cell phone now up to her ear, her other hand pointing at the car as she bent down to look underneath the car. The whole scene looked weird but she was strikingly attractive and her body looked tight. The blouse she had on was stretched a little from her breasts and her ass looked round and tight. If I was a normal citizen I would do what the latest billboards said – *if you see something say something.* I hadn't been normal in years. I got out of my car and walked over to the lady walking around the brand new car. As I got closer I saw that the dark colored vehicle was one of the latest luxury cars. I tried not to startle her.

"Excuse me Miss, do you need help with something." I asked.

"Girl, hold on! I'm sorry I don't have any spare change." She snarled.

"I'm not looking for spare change. You look like you need help."

"Do you work here?"

"I don't have to work here to offer help to a lady." I replied.

"Cute, but I'm fine." She said and waved me off.

"Are you looking for the gas cap?" I asked.

She told whoever she was talking to that she'd call them back and turned to me.

"Look, I appreciate it but I don't need any help."

"It doesn't appear that way to me. You're circling a brand new car, waving your hands and having a screaming conversation with someone." I said.

"You don't know what you're talking about." She snapped back.

"Look! May I open the driver's door to check for a latch or button?" I asked.

"Are you serious? Do I look that stupid?" She asked.

I stood there and let her answer her own question. I heard a horn beep and I turned to see a city utility truck passing by on Los Feliz Boulevard with a familiar face driving. It was Townsend. He nodded and didn't slow his speed.

"I guess you can. I don't think this is necessary though." She said.

She unlocked her vehicle and I looked inside feeling around the floorboard for the gas tank release. I lifted the latch and heard something outside open. When I stood back up I saw her standing there with her arms folded and looking away. Embarrassed I presumed but I wasn't in the mood to rub it in. I bid her a good night and started walking back towards my less attractive set of wheels.

"Hey! Wait…Sir." She yelled.

"Oh now I'm a Sir and no longer looking for spare change?" I asked.

"I deserve that. But you can't be too sure these days." She said.

I felt my cell phone buzzing in my pocket. I didn't excuse myself I just answered it.

"Are you over you childish rant?" Townsend asked.

"Thanks for coming." I said.

Townsend just hung up. I looked back at the rude lady who didn't know her own car and told her it's no problem I should have minded my own business. This is Los Angeles after all. She extended a business card to me and asked if she could buy me a cup of coffee or tea. I didn't take her business card immediately.

"Come on, I really shouldn't have judged you. Take my card. Please." She pleaded.

"I'm normally not a Good Samaritan. So don't worry about it." I told her and started to walk away.

I heard her heels walking across the gas station pavement.

"Sir! Seriously here's my card." She grabbed my left hand and placed her card inside it. She turned and walked back to her car without saying another word. I looked down at the heavy card stock she placed in my hand as she walked back to her vehicle. Her name was Althea Farmingham. She worked in one of the federal buildings in downtown Los Angeles. I put her card in my back pocket and headed back to my vehicle. Henderson called and said he was on Los Feliz Boulevard. I gave him my address and told him I would be waiting at the Chevron gas station.

Henderson called and told me he was pulling up to the house now and there were two black and whites out front with four cops present.

"What exactly am I looking for in this place?" he asked.

"When you get inside you need to go to my office. I will walk you through from there." I told him.

He hung up. I called Townsend to see where he was exactly. He told me he was three houses down and just saw a potbelly detective pull up and talking to two of the police officers. He asked how long did I want him to stay there? I told him until he saw Henderson walk out with a duffle bag. Townsend didn't reply and hung up. He was always about the business. He was never for the fluffy emotional talk. Henderson was buzzing my phone. He had made it inside I walked him through my house slowly and told him to go to my office. When he got to my office I told him there would be a dark colored desk and underneath the center drawer there was a button. Once he pushed the button a sliding door behind him would open. Behind that door was my inventory of weapons and all the cash to my name. The real test would be once I gave him the combination to the safe. What would he do once he walked back outside? I held the phone as I heard Henderson make his way through.

"Damn Lance, you've made a better living than most criminals."

"Henderson, let's not turn this into a phone interview. Get in and get out."

"I'm just about to the office."

"What did you tell the officers outside?"

"I was here to gather some evidence."

"They didn't offer to escort you?"

"I'm a detective! I don't need a fucking escort. Don't piss me off Lance."

I didn't reply to his unnerving response. I needed him to remain focus.

"Ok! I'm inside your office. Nice artwork."

"Thanks! Do you see the desk?"

"Yes. I'm walking over to it now."

"When the sliding door opens the combination to the safe is 31-9-12."

"What's inside exactly?"

"I need you to get all the cash you see."

"Where am I supposed to put *this cash?* "

"There should be two or three black duffle bags on the floor next to the safe."

"Let me open the safe."

I waited as Henderson entered the code to my freedom and my life. I heard him scream *Holy Shit.* I called his name but he didn't answer. Just then Townsend was calling in. I called Henderson's name again but he didn't respond. I clicked over to take Townsend's call.

"Lance, one of the police officers is walking towards the front door. What is your guy doing in there? Do I need to step in?" He asked.

"Wait! No Townsend! We can't afford a blood bath right now. Stand by!"

I clicked back over and yelled for Henderson.

"Yeah Lance I'm here. How much do you think is in here?"

"Should be close to $2 million or a little more."

"Are you serious? Who keeps this kind of money in a safe?"

"I am a criminal remember? Take it all and head out. One of the police officers is walking towards the front door."

"How do you know that?"

"You didn't think I'd let you walk into my place alone did you?

"So you don't trust me?" he laughed.

"You're a crooked detective and I'm on the run. My trust meter isn't exactly glaring at the moment. Hurry up!"

"Anything else you need?" he asked.

"There's no time after your scenic tour. The officer is close to the door. Get out of there."

I heard Henderson zip up the duffle bag and start walking. He coughed and cleared his throat. The phone line went silent then I heard some muffled conversation. Henderson was talking to the officer. I couldn't make out what was being said. Townsend was calling again.

"Lance, I don't trust this pig!"

"Calm down, he's good."

"You're too damn emotional right now. Let me follow this creep and put him to bed.

"No Townsend, just be patient."

I clicked back to the other line without saying goodbye to Townsend. I heard Henderson calling my name repeatedly. I told him I was on the line.

"Where did you go?" He asked.

Ignoring his inquiry I asked him if he had the duffle bag?

"Yes I do. Now what?"

"There's a Scottish pub on the other side of 5 Freeway. Meet me there in 10 minutes."

"Ok!"

I called Townsend and told him to follow Henderson and if Henderson got on the 5 freeway to kill him as quick as he could and get the duffle bag in his possession. Townsend sounded chipper to hear the instructions and I could hear in his voice the hope of the crooked detective taking a detour. I started my car and left the gas station where a not so nice lady gave me her business card.

Traffic was picking up but I wasn't worried about Henderson getting away. I had one of the best trailing him. After we settled up I needed to find Catalina. Hopefully she was still alive. As I pulled up to the bar I saw Henderson parked on the side of the black painted building with the growing green ivy down the sides. The parking lot had three other cars and I could see the city utility truck towards the back of the parking lot. I pulled up on the side of Henderson and motioned for him to get into my car. I saw him take a long draw from his cigarette and flick the cigarette butt then exit his black unmarked car. When he got out he lifted the duffle bag and I told him to put in the back seat. After he tossed the duffle bag on the floor in the backseat he sat in the front seat and began the interrogation.

"So my friend what's your next move?"

"We're not friends!"

"You know what I mean."

"I have a few things left to do that don't concern you. Is there any lost bills laying around in your company issued car?"

He looked at me with a straight face and said no while revealing his 9 MM holstered just under his left shoulder. I made a smirk before asking him if he'd like to get a drink. Before accepting my invitation he asked about his cut for trespassing and tampering with a police investigation. I laughed at his self-righteous temperament all the while asking for some of my blood money. I got out of my car and opened the duffle bag sitting on the backseat. I placed my weapon on the seat as I unzipped what most people worked thirty years to accumulate took less than 8 years. I pulled out 2 ten thousand stacks to give to Henderson. His eyes lit up like a child on Christmas morning. I even saw his hands shaking a little as I placed the money in his grasp. I paid him a compliment I rarely tell anyone – Thank you. He nodded and proceeded to exit the vehicle. I closed the door to my vehicle and asked again about joining me for a drink. Henderson turned and faced me slowly, staring me up and down in silence.

"Lance, there's a special place for people like you. I'll pass on the drink. Be careful out here. Every law enforcement agency is looking for you."

"I can't wait to get to that special place." I said.

I turned and headed towards the front door of one of my old spots. I heard the engine of Henderson's car start and the transmission change gear. And just like that, twenty grand later he was gone. I saw Townsend exit the utility truck and walk towards the front of the parking lot. When I walked in there were 5 patrons sipping on their spirit of choice. The bartender, Milo was drying a shot glass. When we made eye contact he immediately recognized me and stopped drying the glass. I didn't come any further inside the establishment. After about fifteen seconds Milo gave me the nod that indicated it was cool to be there. A much different experience than the overzealous barista gave me. By the time I reached the bar, Milo was in front of me with a stern face. He dried his hands then extended his right hand. A firm embrace exchanged between a law abiding citizen and criminal on the run. Milo looked over towards Townsend then back at me.

"Is he with you?" He asked.

"Yes Milo he is."

Milo released my hand and asked me what was I having. I told him a double shot of Macallan 25. He then asked Townsend the same. He told Milo he'd have a rum and diet coke with a lime. Milo smiled and before walking away he asked Townsend was this where his tax dollars were going? With a quick reply Townsend told him not even close and sat on the bar stool next to me.

Just as Milo returned with our drinks, the large screen television at the end of the bar cut in with breaking news. Milo immediately reached for the remote on the back counter and turned to a sports channel. He looked at me with a sly smirk and went to check on his other patrons. I hadn't been here in years. Occasionally I'd see Milo around town and he'd always tell me to stop by. The one night I stopped by he wasn't there and with my schedule I never had the chance to stop back by. It was good to know the respect was still there.

"Lance, what's your plan? You don't have a lot of

time?" Townsend asked.

"Maison should be back in a couple of days and he shouldn't be alive much longer after that."

"A couple of days to an upstanding citizen will fly by. But to a criminal on the run that's an awful long time to live on the run in the same area. What about this kid cop?"

"I hear you!" I said.

"Do you? Who was the lady you were talking to at the gas station? You don't have time for romance!"

"If I'm keeping you from something, you're free to leave anytime. But I have this under control." I told him.

"Save your cop out pleas for someone else. I didn't come this far to get into a pissing contest with you. Finish this shit and get your life back!"

Townsend finished his mixed drink and placed a fifty-dollar bill on the counter and stepped away from the bar towards the door. Just before he pushed the door to exit he yelled across the small bar room "you know where to find me and get your ass someplace low and safe". Before leaving he made eye contact with Milo and nodded his head in appreciation of the loyal patronage to me. One last look at me then he walked out. Milo and the other customers were looking my way. I turned to face them but I could feel their eyes piercing through my body like x-ray vision. I continued sitting there enjoying my scotch and admiring all of the worldly spirits Milo had available for anyone looking to get away from their nightmare of reality. I knew Townsend was right but I wanted to do this my way. For the way Maison played me I wanted to truly make him suffer like a starving drug addict looking for their next hit. Thad would be a quick to the point death. His immaturity irritated me and him thinking I actually owed him something was a running joke in my head and made me chuckle to myself. Milo came by and asked if I wanted another scotch. The double shot I ordered was just enough to soothe my soul and dull my senses a bit. I kindly declined and told him thanks for the warm hospitality. I stepped down from my bar stool and headed to the door that Townsend used.

"Lance!"

I turned and acknowledged Milo.

"Take care of yourself and if you need anything just say the word."

"Thanks Milo."

The thought never entered my mind. The last recruit didn't work out so I didn't want to corrupt Milo's life. As I walked towards my car I had this strange feeling that the windows were busted out and the duffle bag was gone.

Each step closer my legs started to feel weak and my pace slowed. I felt my palms starting to sweat. My mind was racing faster than a favored pony at the Kentucky Derby. I heard a car horn from the boulevard and I drew my 9mm and quickly turned around with the barrel pointed straight ahead. The parking lot was empty and traffic on the boulevard was moving steady. No one was worried about my pathetic ass, at least not at this moment. I unlocked my car and grabbed the duffle bag and placed it on the floor of the passenger side. I started up my only means of transportation and headed towards the city of Carson. I exited the parking lot and entered the on ramp of the 5 Freeway South and turned to the old school radio station. The disc jockey was playing something funky from the early 80s – Skin Tight by the Ohio Players. My uncle used to play this on his 8 track player with his old pals. They used to hang out in his backyard drinking moonshine and lying. My memories of my cousins were more enjoyable than those of my immediate family. Funny how family relationships worked? Just as the song was ending the radio blasted sirens. I immediately knew the next song coming into play – Fire. I didn't know who the disc jockey was but he had the So Cal radio waves grooving and anyone in their car listening was definitely car dancing. I wasn't sure where I was headed but I merged onto the 110 freeway. At first I thought about heading to Santa Monica but I felt the owners were more like family and I would feel terrible if their motel of generations were in the news for harboring a savage like me on the run. I pulled out the business card given to me by the stranger at the gas station. I didn't pay her much attention but her smile caught my attention and I saw it when I looked at her business card. I dropped it in the middle console and accelerated to my unknown destination.

Townsend sent me a text and asked if I was ok and somewhere out of the spotlight. I replied and told him I was ok but still looking for a place to lay low for the night. He sent another text and told me to get some place fast because every local news station was reporting on my unknown whereabouts and L.A.P.D is offering a $50,000 reward for any information on my whereabouts. I didn't reply to his last text message. At that moment I knew where I needed to go at least for the night. I stayed on the 110 freeway towards the city of Carson. When I reached the 91 freeway I took the eastbound ramp. Just off of the Avalon Boulevard exit opposite the eastbound exit was a hole in the wall motel. I found it years ago when I first got into this profitable yet heartless line of business. I was chasing down a local drug dealer and this hotel was where he'd meet his many runners for mobile deposits. The motel was nothing fancy at all. There was no front desk or plush lounge. Just a bulletproof glass with a small slot for you to receive the key after you filled out the small 3" x 5" card with the spurious information. Cash was the normal form of payment leaving no trace of identity. When I turned into the narrow parking lot I saw five cars in the parking lot. At least three rooms were occupied and committing morally wrong acts of sexual congress. The person working behind the heavy glass was an older man of Indian decent wearing cologne so heavy I could smell it through the thick glass. There was a small television on the counter showing an Indian program. There was no greeting. He quickly looked up at me then slid the small card and a worn black pen under the small slot. I filled it out as countless others before me had done and placed it back in the slot. He didn't ask me for identification as he reached for a key on the board inside his puny office. In his heavy Indian dialect he told me $69.99 plus tax. I slid a hundred dollar bill and he returned $21.00 then he slid the key under the slot and went back to watching his television program. He didn't bother to tell me the check-out time or when breakfast was offered. In this setting no one stayed overnight. It was a cash exchange for quick criminal acts or an exchange of guilty pleasures or both.

When I unlocked the door to room 2 I could hear the noise from the next room to the left of me releasing their sins. It sounded like one party was close to being sinfully cleansed while the other was still repenting. I didn't disturb their session by tapping on the wall. I dropped my duffle bags on the floor as I scrutinized the surroundings I had been reduced to. The walls were covered in pale flowery wallpaper. The carpet was chocolate brown with cigarette burns throughout. The bed looked to be a full size with a sunken mattress. I sat on it and felt the worn out springs. I didn't have time to run to Walmart and pick up an egg crate foam cover. A rotted wood nightstand with water spots and cigarette markings was next to the bed with a skinny lamp and a dingy white cover with frayed material. The good book was inside the drawer of the nightstand and some menus. Across from the bed was an old wooden six-drawer dresser with a small television. I walked across the stained carpet to the bathroom to take a shower. Inside the unpretentious water closet was a small sink with a cracked vanity mirror. The shower tub had a pale blue shower curtain hanging from the rusted shower rod and inside the tub I saw a few rusted water spots. I turned on the hot water then the cold before turning the handle for the shower. The hot water reached a warm temperature and remained there. I turned the cold water off. Before getting in the shower I caught of glimpse of myself in the damaged vanity. As the water came out of the shower head I thought about my next move, Catalina and the business card inside the middle console of my vehicle. My mind was trying to get me back in the ring of love. I shook my head refusing to give in. I couldn't prolong the deaths of two deserving bastards. I washed up under the warm water and put on some fresh sweats before powering up the laptop. I needed to see if Maison had taken the bait of me going to Omaha or if his arrogance would concede when it came to his only child alive. When I logged into the tracking database it showed no activity on his credit cards and three calls made from his cell phone. His passport didn't show an exit stamp from Turkey and re-entry stamp into the United States. What an arrogant prick. I logged out and typed in another website. It was the latest site for men and women's guilty pleasures. Women as well as men were calling escorts to outcall destinations and paying the fee for intimate discretion. The website was for the elite and required a background check before anyone traveled to your secluded location. Each profile had disclaimers of independence and no affiliation with law enforcement. The profiles looked professionally done with black or white backdrops. No selfies from a bathroom or leaning up against a wall. The categories available could meet the need of anyone in search of intimate company. I clicked on the Ebony section and 14 women with green dots by their profile indicating *available* were at my fingertips. I scrolled through like I was reading the wanted ads in the Sunday paper. As I viewed the profiles of these beautiful women I couldn't help but wonder how they ended up in this line of work. But then what did it say about me for even being on the website. What did I care if some woman had no problem selling her body? I clicked on the profile of a dark skin woman with twists age 24 by the name of Mahogany. Her profile said she was 5'0 and 125 lbs. Her body appeared tone as she posed for the photographer in seductive workout gear. She definitely couldn't walk into a gym with that on. Her eyes were big and her eyelashes appeared to be long, if they weren't fake. In one of her poses her assets looked firm and round. I didn't see any body markings. Her hourly rate wasn't cheap and said outcalls to upscale hotels, no residences. I had to consider my environment and hoped she'd even take the outcall. I dialed the number in her profile and after 5 rings an automated voice answered and told callers to leave their name and number for Mahogany to get back to you. I followed the instructions.

As I sat in the unappealing room waiting for the online profile to call back I heard two of the cars start up and leave. Sexual confessions had ended for the night. Since Maison hadn't made it back I needed to get going on Thad to keep me busy. I pulled up his information to see if he still lived in his one bedroom apartment on 47th Street and Normandie Avenue; it was a four apartment building with two upstairs and two on the ground floor. Thad lived in one of the upstairs units. He was currently out on bail with a court date in a couple of weeks. If everything went as planned he'd never make it to his trial but a courtroom based on his confessions and repentance. Neither was my concern.

I was interrupted by an incoming call from what I presumed was Mahogany.

"Hello." I said.

"Who's speaking?" The soft voice inquired.

I almost said my Government name.

"Patrick."

"Do you have a last name Patrick?"

I looked at the phony ID.

"Green."

"What can I do for you Mr. Green?"

"Looking for some company. Are you available?"

"Where are you sweetie?"

And just like the transaction began.

"I'm in Carson."

"Are you at the Doubletree or Embassy Suites?"

"No I'm at a small place off the 91 Freeway."

"Only upscale hotels sweetie."

"I understand but I'm in town on business and got in late. This was all that was available close to my meeting in the morning." I lied.

"What's your driver's license number sweetie?"

I read her the numbers of the ID in my hand. She repeated the numbers and asked me to hold on. I heard the elevator music as I held the line while a phony ID was having a background check run. When she returned to the line she told me her rate would be double. I ran the numbers based on how long I wanted her company.

"$2,800.00. No problem."

"What is the address sweetie? I can be there in an hour."

I gave the soft seductive sounding voice the address and room number of my hideaway. She told me she'd see me soon. When we disconnected I looked around the

$69.99 + tax room and shook my head at how evil the almighty dollar really was and what people would do to get it. I laughed at myself thinking of the risk I was taking having a stranger come to fulfill my lustful wants in such meager accommodations. I unzipped the duffle bag and took out enough to pay Mahogany and put the duffle bag under the bed towards the middle. I lifted the depleted mattress and put the laptops underneath. I turned on the television set and surprisingly it had cable and a clear picture. I flipped through the channels until I found the sports channel to watch the day's highlights.

I heard a car pull up outside and soon a knock at my door. As I approached the door I could hear the engine of the car still running. When I opened the door I saw Mahogany standing there and the black Lincoln town car pulled off once I was verified as Patrick Green. At least that's who she thought I was. Her skin was dark and rich like Colombian coffee beans. I could smell her fragrance and it immediately put me in a trance. Her profile credentials were exact and I was mesmerized by her twists. I wanted to touch them but she extended her hand and said it was a pleasure to meet me. Then she hugged me and came into the paltry room. I could see the look of distaste and apprehensiveness on her makeup free face. I could tell the tight jeans she donned were costly and her silk blouse had a designer's name attached to it without a doubt. The 4 inch pumps she wore hadn't stepped on anything but expensive carpet and exotic floors. The builder's grade carpet beneath her fancy pumps was an insult and the room was a backhand slap against her face. The silence was broken when she saw the dead Presidents on the cheap desk.

"Sweetie, let me slip out of these jeans and give you a massage."

I watched as she walked over to collect her service fee. She placed the stack of currency in her purse and began undressing. As she unbuttoned her blouse I could see her deep purple bra holding her D cups and her stomach wasn't flat but it wasn't fat either. When she pulled her denim jeans down her thighs they were muscular and tight. The matching thong was fitting nicely around her waist. I could see a hint of bare skin around her holy grounds. Her dark coated skin was flawless and tattoo free. I tried to remain in the moment but I was truly mystified that this woman was in this line of work. I almost broke the unwritten rule and inquired but I didn't get a chance because she interrupted my therapeutic inner self. Mahogany pulled out a small bottle of massage oil and a handful of condoms from her purse before walking over to the bed. She moved the top spread back to the foot of the bed and motioned for me to come and lay down.

As I walked over she had her right index finger resting over her lips sizing me up. My thoughts had already drifted to how much of my anger and pain I was going to take out on her. I hadn't been with a woman in months and I wasn't sure how my injuries would hold up. When I walked up to her she didn't waste any time pulling my shirt over my head. She looked at my chest and rubbed her hands across my old wounds. She didn't ask about the bandage. Her touch became more firm when she reached my waist area and I flinched a little. A slight pain was still present.

"Is that too rough?" She asked in a sincere lying voice.

"No! It's fine."

"Are you sure?"

"Yes!"

Her hands were soft and smooth as she unbuttoned my pants and slid them down my legs. When she stood back up she couldn't help but notice my hard erection. She licked her lips as she took him into her warm hands. She stroked him and never lost eye contact with me. The way she massaged my dick was like no other hand job I'd ever felt. She knelt down and took my balls into her mouth. Her tongue was lethal as she juggled my balls gently in her mouth. She pushed me back onto to the bed and took the tip of my dick into her mouth. Her lips were full, hot and wet. Her strokes were slow but long against the shaft of my dick. She licked it up and down along the sides while still massaging him with her hand. I reached for her firm breasts and she moaned seductively from my touch. Her tongue played with the tip of my dick like it was a friendly game of one lick; two lick how many licks until the creamy center explodes. After a few more wet licks, my paid by the hour employee stood up. She unsnapped her bra and her firm breasts stayed in place. Her areola was just as dark as her rich skin and her nipples were slightly erect. As she slowly slid her thong down her tight thighs I saw her shaved pussy and a glowing pink entry way.

"Turn over Patrick!" She commanded.

I had momentarily forgotten my fake identification before turning over.

"You have a nice ass." She said.

Another lie I didn't respond to. I felt her warm body climb onto me as her warm hands applied the non-scented oil and began massaging my back. I could feel her warm pussy resting in the small of my back. She continued rubbing my cursed body and kissed the back of my neck down my spine stopping just before my *nice* ass. Then I felt all of her laying on me as she kissed me behind my left ear. The treatment felt amazing and reminded me of the ancient Nuru massage. I heard her whisper a rehearsed lie into my ear telling me how strong I felt before she got off of me. Mahogany reached for one of the condoms and proceeded to unroll the love glove down the shaft of my dick. Unfortunately, there wasn't any love in this room. This was a precautionary measure of safe sex and no trust. Real love didn't require such safety measures. Real love didn't exist in my world or hers. My DNA was still a virgin to procreation and a permanent resident of the local sewer system.

Mahogany took one last look at the love glove before she slid slowly down onto my rod of steel. Her moist pink center was tight as she adjusted to her latest scene of seduction. Her dishonest moans entered the stale room and her hips began to show me what I had paid for. Her eyes were closed as she pretended to be in ecstasy. She had acted out this same scene many times before me and the show wouldn't end after me. Mahogany would move on to the next director soon after our scene was complete. I laid there and listen to her well paid deceptive tongue whisper lies of seduction.

"Oh sweetie you feel so good. How do you want it? Your wish is Mahogany's command."

"Ride slow and bounce on my dick!"

"Yes sweetie."

She leaned forward and raised her hips then rode my dick better than a triple Preakness jockey. Her chocolate D cups were bouncing right before my eyes. I reached for one of them and squeezed it hard enough to interrupt her moans. She didn't tell me to stop. She couldn't. I had paid for what I wanted and how I wanted it. The only rule in this hedonistic room was the love glove. As she continued riding me I grabbed her neck turning her moans into short gasps for air. Her fascinating hip movement didn't stop and she tried to speak in between my grip.

"You like it rough sweetie? Punish me I've been naughty all week."

There was probably some truth to that. I removed my hand from her neck and grabbed a handful of her twists. They were hers I could tell because my grip was strong enough to pull out a few tracks of India's finest. I grabbed her hips to control the tempo as my dick went in deeper. I could feel her wetness all over the love glove and I wondered if someone could hear my sinful confessions.

"Patrick, I'm about to cum sweetie. Damn you're

working my chocolate pussy."

I played along with the lies.

"Am I? Does your pussy feel good?"

"Yes daddy, so damn good. Don't stop."

Her wish was my command. I flipped her off of me onto her side and slid back inside of her. Her eyes remained closed as I worked my young evening delight. I smacked her ass hard enough to leave a welt. My thrust was so powerful I could feel her easing up the bed. Her moans continued to invade the sinful air and her tongue enticed me more.

"Come on Patrick don't be stingy with the dick. I told you I've been naughty. Make me pay for being such a bad girl."

"How bad have you been?"

Her eyes opened for the first time and she looked at me and said "real bad!"

I turned Mahogany over onto her back and pressed her legs back until they were by her ears and slid back into her pink canal. I looked at this young girl laying here and take this perverse treatment with no sentiment at all. As I slammed into her youthful but experienced pussy all I could see was the torture being administered to Maison. I grabbed her neck again and she being the great actress played right along and told me how good it felt.

"Put me on my hands and knees Patrick!"

Her low erotic voice was starting to turn me on. I pulled my dick out of her and did what she asked. Her dark chocolate ass was firm and dimple free. She knew the position too well as she rested comfortably on her elbows anticipating my knock at her dripping wet pussy lips. With one hand around her hips I wasted no time getting back to pleasure and pain. My strokes were filled with nefarious thoughts. I reached down and grabbed her arms pulling her firm backside into my pelvic area. I envisioned I was a power tool working at the max load capacity. I let her arms go and she fell onto her elbows then I grabbed a handful of her twists and made her back arch as my stroke continued invading her sinful playground. My stroke was interrupted by a series of beeps on the nightstand. It wasn't her timer indicating my sessions had ended. It was an important message waiting for me. I started pounding her pussy once more resting my tight grip around her hips.

"That's it Patrick, take this pussy. Hit it like you want it, hit it for it's worth to you."

She was a devil in living flesh. No one had ever told me to punish them like this. I continued sliding in and out of her wet pussy. Our bodies were drenched in salty sweat.

She told me she was reaching another climax and I felt mine approaching. She started bouncing her firm cheeks up against me and pulling my dick. Her hips were magical as she continued working my dick until I exploded inside the love glove. She pulled away from me and took the love glove off and licked around the tip of my dick getting the last of my sperm. When she finished she got out of bed and grabbed her personal things and went into the bathroom. I sat on the side of the bed thinking about the message waiting for me on the nightstand.

I reached for the cell phone and viewed the message. My blood immediately started to boil and I clenched my fists tightly. I felt my cheekbones tighten as I read the message -

Maison Chambers has re-entered the United States. He just cleared customs in the Tom Bradley International Terminal at LAX.

When Mahogany returned from the bathroom I was dressed and just as anxious for her to leave. She pulled out her cell phone and called for her late night chariot. While we both waited impatiently there was no conversation and no eye contact. When I heard the engine outside pull up I opened the door for her but didn't thank her or bid her good night. The business transaction was over and I didn't want a receipt for services received. As she walked by to the door, she offered a plain white business card with her name and phone number with the caption '*for serious bookings*' only. I kindly declined and told her I wouldn't be in town much longer. She frowned a bit. I suppose rejection wasn't normal in her line of work. When I saw the brake lights disappear at the end of the narrow drive way I gathered all of my gear and headed for the door. I needed better digs than this to concentrate on Maison. I wouldn't be able to drive to Calabasas and politely ask him to come with me. I took one last look around the room and pulled the door of room 2 shut. I looked at my watch. It was just after 2 AM in the morning. I pulled out my cell phone and called the number of a homely hotel in the revived little Tokyo in downtown Los Angeles.

"Thank you for calling the Miyuki Hotel, Benji speaking."

"It's been a while Benji. How have you been?" I asked.

"May I ask who's speaking?" He asked.

"It's your old friend the print man." I said.

"Well hello Sir! It has been quite a while. How may I

assist you?"

"I need a suite for a few weeks on a high floor."

"When would you be checking in?"

"I'm en route!"

"Let me check for you Sir."

From the first time I met Benji at a security conference he was a professional. He never forgot your name but never mentioned it after meeting you. It was 'sir' or 'my friend' thereafter. He returned back to the line and told me the hotel could accommodate the days I needed and he would be waiting for me when I checked in. I entered the 91 Freeway west and connected to the 110 Freeway north. The Miyuki was located a few blocks from Maison's main building and in the center of a lot of tourist activities; a place I could get lost in the crowd while I put Maison's death into works. Freeway accessibility was nearby as well. I pulled up in front of the hotel and the parking attendant met me and asked me if I needed help with my luggage. I told him thank you but declined his assistance. When I walked into the hotel, the lobby was different than I had remembered. It had a new look to it with contemporary furniture, water fountains, dark painted walls and Japanese writings throughout. There was a small business center with the latest trendy flat screen monitors and sleek keyboards. I could see Benji was still maintaining his 6'3" petite frame. His fade haircut was fresh and his line in the front was razor sharp. His hotel uniform was wrinkle free and snug to his small frame. When I approached the front counter he greeted me as if we'd just seen each other yesterday. We griped hands and bumped shoulders. Then it was all business. He asked for my check in credentials and I presented my new identity information. He glanced at it and back at me quickly but never said a word or showed any uneasiness. Benji swiped my credit card and ran down the checklist of things he told other guests about the hotel as they checked in. It meant nothing to me, this wasn't a vacation and I knew all of the local attractions. He told me my suite number and gave me the key card to my room. As I headed to the elevators Benji came from behind the counter.

"Sir, I will turn your do not disturb on and let you know if you receive any messages."

I stood there in the foyer looking at my old colleague. What he just confirmed was he had seen the news and was aware of my situation. Unsolicited loyalty could be a gift and a curse. For now I had to trust that Benji was a gift. I would really know shortly after I got to my suite or in the morning when I woke up. Either I'd walk through the lobby as a normal hotel guest getting some morning brew or Thad's fraternal order in blue would be waiting for me quietly by the coffee station with the cream and sugar.

Before I fell asleep I sent Townsend a text message.

"I'm in a safe place for a few nights"

He replied right away.

"Glad to hear that. The news coverage about you has increased. I may have a lead on Catalina's whereabouts." He said.

"Where is she?" I replied.

"Where is Maison and the young kid cop?"

"Maison just returned to the U.S. I'm not sure about Thad."

"Then Catalina shouldn't concern you. Take the breath away from those two, then worry about Catalina."

"Townsend! Where is Catalina?" I texted.

"I can see how you got caught slipping! Tighten up Lance. Get some rest and handle your business."

I was done texting. I dialed his number but he didn't answer. I called again and the phone went straight to voicemail. I sent him another text asking him to pick up the phone. I knew he wasn't going to. He was the epitome of stubborn.

I got up and headed to the bathroom to enjoy a hot

shower. As the water flowed through the showerhead my mind drifted to two women. One I had known for a decade and grown to love as my mother. The other was a stranger with a nasty attitude but something about her peak my interest. I knew deep down inside I needed to make a decision to either kill two people or take the cash I had and leave town and never look back. But mentally I didn't feel able to do either one until I knew the status of Catalina. If I knew she was dead at least then I'd know but the 'unknown' was killing me. Townsend's reluctance to give me information wasn't helping. I may have to stop communicating with him altogether until I tell him I've killed two people or I've decided not to and I'm leaving town. Thoughts of Althea clouded my head because if I left town and didn't kill those two people what would my chances be of her falling in love with me; a killer? How could I convince her to leave her career behind to follow me? The title underneath her name didn't say administrative assistant. She had either put in some hard work and dedication or slept her way into the position. Either way I doubt she would leave it so freely. I turned the shower off and step onto the marble tile. My reflection in the mirror was disgusting to my sight. I was pathetic and felt ashamed of my entire being. The decisions I battled with should have been no brainers. Townsend had come to my rescue. A crooked detective broke the law and entered my residence under police watch to get the only money I had to my name. But still I couldn't walk away. My insides burned when I thought of how Maison used me. I could leave without killing Thad but I would be watching my back the rest of my life. The disgusting face was still sharing at me. I cracked my knuckles and twisted my neck slightly to the left as my mental psyche confirmed what needed to be done. No more second thoughts. I got into my hotel bed and stirred around for a few minutes more before falling asleep.

I woke up in a bed of sweat from my normal sleep pattern; a nightmare. I was tied to a chair in an old building and the lower part of my body was being dipped into a barrel of acid. I felt my skin falling off and excruciating pain. I could hear myself screaming as the group of unknown people lowered and raised the chair. Each time I came out of the sizzling barrel I wiggled and tried to escape the rope tied around my wrists. I couldn't break free as my body went in for another acidic cleansing. My yells were unanswered as the faceless torturers continued doing what I had done for years. I got up and washed my face in cold water and brushed my teeth so hard, still in anger from my dreadful nightmare that someday just may become a reality. I finished getting dressed and headed downstairs.

When I got to the lobby, breakfast was being served in a small area off from the lobby. I saw European and Asian tourists getting croissants and omelets made. I found a small table facing a big pane window before getting some fruit, oatmeal and coffee. Just before I left the coffee area I heard a plate break on the floor. I immediately knelt down and reached for my gun but didn't expose it. My continental breakfast spilled in front of me. One of the hotel staff members came over to clean up my mess but I told her it was okay. The older looking woman continued picking up the spilled pieces of fruit as I wiped up the oatmeal.

"I recognize you Sir." She said.

I froze right there. I couldn't speak.

"It's okay I'm not going to ask for your autograph. We're not allowed to bother guest during their stay." She continued.

"I'm sorry. You must be mistaking. I'm not a celebrity ma'am." I told her.

"Oh sure you are. I've seen most of your movies. My favorite is the one where you played a football player." She smiled.

I didn't know who she thought I was but my nerves were back to normal. She told me she'd get me a new bowl of oatmeal and fruit and asked if I wanted some more coffee. I told her yes and walked back to my table. When I sat down I took a deep breath and looked around the small area assessing everyone. I looked over to the front counter but Benji's shift was over. A young bubbly white woman was working the counter and saying good morning to everyone. The hotel staff member came to my table and dropped off my breakfast. I thanked her and she smiled and continued helping the other hotel guests. I looked out into the busy streets of downtown L.A. as the W-2 employees scurried to get their fancy lattes and then to their modern day slave jobs. Maison's main high rise was a few blocks away. From where I was sitting I could see the corner of it. A new towering hotel was across the street and the old place where I met Jordan was in my view. I started eating my breakfast as I pulled out Althea's business card and dialed the number at the bottom. As the phone began to ring a feeling of nervousness took over my body all of sudden. The phone stopped ringing after 2 rings. I wasn't ready.

"Althea Farmingham speaking."

I mustered up enough energy to say good morning.

"Who's speaking?"

"This is Patrick."

A short pause before she spoke again.

"Oh yes Patrick. I'm glad you called. I'm really sorry for the other night."

"It's okay. I should've minded my own business."

"No! I really appreciate you helping me. How are you?"

"I'm doing well. Would you like to have lunch today?"

I was never a fan of the small talk. She told me her day was pretty full but she would check with her assistant. She asked if the number I was calling from was a good number. I supposed it was until I felt it was compromised like the previous ones I had tossed. I told her that it was. Althea pleasantly told me she would get back to me and we said goodbye. After we hung up I literally exhaled and felt my heart slow down from the record breaking pace it was beating. I needed to ditch the sweats and t-shirt look I had been wearing since I left the hospital.

I finished my breakfast and left a tip along with a scribbled name on the napkin for the hostess. At least I would put a smile on someone's face today. I walked out of the hotel and headed to the garment district to see an old friend who had a premier clothing store for men. Along the way I walked by Maison's all glass building. I hadn't been near it since I started following Jordan's brother. I saw many people going in and out of the building. It was a busy place and would be nearly impossible to nab him from here. I continued on to the garment district as the flow along the sidewalks steadily increased with people. Being downtown felt good even if I wasn't supposed to be there. The air, the smell of the mom and pop restaurants, the people and the horn honkers; it was a scene that would never get old because every day was different. I passed by the bank where I made my last withdrawal and stupid plea to be with a woman. I felt my cell phone vibrating in my pocket. I pulled it out and the number was a 213 area code. I hesitantly answered it hoping Thad hadn't tracked this number.

"Hello!"

"Hi Patrick! It's Althea."

With all of the outside noise I could barely hear her.

"How's it going?"

"Good I was calling to tell you I could meet for lunch today around noon if you're available."

"Noon is fine, where would you like to meet?"

"Are you familiar with downtown L.A.?"

"I'm sure I can find wherever you want to meet."

"There's a Salvadorian restaurant on 3rd street. It's small but the food is delicious."

"See you there at noon."

"Okay Patrick. Have a good morning."

"Thanks."

I hadn't been on a date in so long it felt weird confirming the meeting time. When I arrived in front of the old building front on 7th street it looked run down and abandoned. I walked inside and started up the steps to the 3rd floor where I last knew Zad to be. When I reached the 3rd floor I didn't see his store. Someone else was there. I looked around and they could tell I was lost.

"Can I help you?"

"Yeah is Zad's no longer in business?" .

He said something in Russian I believe to the other guy sitting with him. The other guy pointed down and then threw his hands up in the air.

"Zad moved to the 1st floor."

"Thanks!"

I walked back downstairs and looked around and he was there in the back corner. I saw him sitting reading the newspaper with a small ceramic cup next to him. He always drank coffee from Peru, black no cream and no sugar. He had aged a bit and put on a few pounds.

"How's it going Zad?"

He turned my way and revealed his signature smile.

"My friend it's been a long time. How have you been?"

"Trying to survive another day."

"Yes I see that. What's this news about you?"

He stood and gave me a hug and kissed my left and right cheek.

"Would you like some coffee?"

"No thanks. How have you been?"

"Blessed my friend. I had to move to the 1st floor because of my freaking back."

"Oh ok. I was worried you had shut down when I didn't see you on the 3rd floor."

"No way my friend! I'm still here. You look the same Lance."

Zad had known me for many years. I attended his daughter's wedding and was by his side when his wife passed away. I didn't mind him calling me by my Government name.

"Zad I need a few pieces. Can you help me?"

"Of course, of course!"

He stood up and walked towards one of his many racks of clothing.

"What size are you now? 32 in the waist and 42 long in jacket?"

"That sounds about right."

"Here try these on."

He pointed towards his fitting room, a 4' x 4' closet with a black curtain for your privacy. When I pulled the curtain. I heard Zad walking towards the fitting room.

"Lance! Are you okay my friend? The news is saying some pretty bad things about you. I don't believe a word of it."

"Yeah Zad I'm okay, just a misunderstanding of the facts. My name will be cleared in due time."

"I hope so. You're like a son to me. From the first time you came into my shop I never asked you any questions you know."

Hearing those words stop me from zipping up the pants I was trying on. "Like a son" those words were lethal and something I'd never heard before. Not even from my biological father.

"Lance?"

"Yeah Zad. Let me finish getting dressed, I'll be right out."

I put the jacket on and pulled the curtain to the side. When I stepped out of the fitting room Zad walked towards me and grabbed the shoulders of the coat and then the sides.

"You should have this taken in. How are the pants?"

"Great. I need a few dress shirts to go with this."

"Yes of course."

When I returned to the front of Zad's store I handed him one of the suits and saw he had picked a few shirts to match and some black lace up dress shoes with black socks.

"Same price?" I asked.

"Same price my friend."

I asked when would the tailoring be finished? He told me around 3 o'clock. I took the dark grey suit and the blue patterned dress shirt along with the dress shoes back to the fitting room. I immediately felt like my old self with the new clothes. I returned to the front where Zad was back in his seat. We shook hands and I told him I'd see him this afternoon. As I headed to the door I heard Zad say "be careful out there son." I turned around and saw his signature smile. There it was again. Within a thirty-minute timeframe I heard the word *son* twice but I hadn't heard it once in the lifetime of my biological father. I told him thank you before pushing the exit bar on the door.

Across the street from Maison's building was a small café. I went in and ordered a small cappuccino and got a seat at the countertop by the window. I picked up the used newspaper next to me and browsed through it. It wasn't too long before I saw Maison pull up in front of his building. Like normal he got out of his car like he didn't have a care in the world and entered the building. He didn't look nervous or threatened by me being free. I looked for some sort of security team to be with him but I didn't see anyone. But I must remember this is the same slimy son of a bitch who had me on a wild goose chase. I pulled out my cell phone and called him. The phone started ringing just as he entered his building.

"Maison here."

"Isn't it a beautiful morning?"

"Who's speaking and how can I help you?"

"I don't suppose you'd turn around and walk back out of your building, would you?"

He stopped walking and turned around. Then walked back to the glass front door and looked around.

"Lance?"

"How'd you guess?"

"You're still a free man?"

"And you're a dead man walking."

"Is that so? You think you're going to walk the streets freely forever?"

"No! Just long enough to kill you!"

"I doubt that very seriously."

I saw him pull out another cell phone but he didn't put it up to his ear. He was texting someone.

"Now that I have your attention, you better move very carefully."

"I'm always careful. Wasn't I careful enough to fool you?"

I wanted to run across the street and pull his throat out of his neck right then. Just then is when I saw two black SUVs pull up with four men in each.

"I was wondering if you had a team of dummies?"

"Dummies?"

"Yes! Their skill set is no match for what's coming your way."

I saw him looking all around trying to place my whereabouts.

"Don't worry about where I am Maison. I will have eyes on you until the last set of eyes you see are mine!"

I disconnected the call and sat there with joy watching him give instructions to his intramural security team. I finished reading the paper and enjoyed my cappuccino before meeting Althea.

As I approached 3rd street I saw Althea walking

towards the El Salvadorian restaurant. She had on a dark skirt suit with a nude color shell underneath with a nude pair of heels. Her hair was just past shoulder length and I couldn't tell if she had on makeup. She appeared very busy on her cell phone. I kept walking towards the restaurant. I felt my cell phone vibrating. I pulled it out of my jacket pocket to see who it was. It was Townsend. I didn't answer. I sent him a text instead and told him I had seen Maison and was going into a meeting. He didn't reply.

When Althea walked into the restaurant she saw me sitting by the front door. She waved and finished up her conversation. I stood up when she got closer to me.

"Hi Patrick! Sorry about that. Work is extremely busy these days."

"No problem."

"Did they say how long the wait was?"

"I didn't ask. I just sat down and waited for you."

She stepped forward to the maitre d.

"Two please by a window if possible."

Her independence was evident. Her walk to the table was confident but not arrogant.

"Is this okay Patrick?"

"It's fine."

"Thank you." She told the maitre d.

"So I'm glad I was able to make it today. I was surprised but happy you called."

"I was surprised I called." I said.

"I know I was a bit rude the other night. I apologize again."

"I'm over it, otherwise we wouldn't be having lunch." I smiled.

"So Mr. Patrick do you work downtown? What line of work are you in?"

She was just like every other woman with the interview questions. I guess that's a part of getting to know a person. Something I wasn't familiar with at all.

"Right now I'm in between jobs and rethinking my methods of business."

"Reassessment is always good."

"Sometimes life leaves you no choice."

"That's true as well."

A young male waiter came to our table and asked to take our drink order. Althea ordered sparkling water. I ordered tap water with a lemon. He went over the daily special and then left to get our drinks.

Althea continued the conversation and started to talk about herself. She said she had moved to Los Angeles 10 years ago with her fiancé, but didn't go through with the marriage. After the breakup she fell in love with her career and went on occasional dates and had a few friends with benefits encounters but that got old and the benefits weren't that good. She laughed out loud. She was originally from Tucson, Arizona and went to Howard University for both undergrad and law school. She said eventually she wanted a family but her biological clock was ticking so adoption might be the viable option. The waiter returned with our drinks and asked if we were ready to order. Neither one of us had looked at the menu but I had been here quite a few times and knew what I wanted.

"Patrick are you ready to order? I'm sorry I started talking so much."

"Sure I'm ready if you are."

"Yes. May I have the lomo saltado."

"For you sir?" The waiter asked.

"I'll take the carne quisada."

The waiter read our orders back to us and moved on to the next table. The lunch crowd was coming in. I pray no one recognizes me.

"So Patrick, what about you? What's your story? How many hearts have you broken?"

I smiled before I responded.

"Why do you think I've broken a lot of hearts."

"Oh come on, a man in L.A. who helps a complete stranger at a gas station? That's not normal. So I know you're a gentleman."

"I'm not from L.A."

"Even better. Where are you from?"

"I'm from North Carolina."

"I heard southern men our good men."

"Do you believe everything you hear?"

"Hell…oops I'm sorry. No I don't." She laughed.

"Well I didn't go to college like you. I enlisted in the Army and picked up a particular set of skills that's help me get through life."

"I thought the Army gave out degrees?"

"No they don't. You learn your job series by attending a military school. But you don't get a degree." I laughed.

"So what did you do in the Army?"

Thank God the waiter came with our orders. Eating our meals would give me some time to stall before I answered her questions. Althea lowered her head and blessed her food silently. When she finished she made a cross over her heart and kissed her fingers afterwards. She was Catholic. I said my simple prayer of *Jesus wept.* Hell I didn't even know Jesus. I had so much blood and sin on my hands, he'd have to set aside a special time and place for my confessions. I didn't make a cross over my heart. Then we began eating our meals.

"So….from North Carolina, went into the Army. Any kids? Ever been married?"

I wiped my mouth and smiled before answering the inquisitive woman sitting across from me. I guess she felt I should be as open as she had been. She really didn't want the truth about Patrick aka Lance.

"I was a computer technician in the Army. No kids. Never been married."

"Were you ever engaged?"

I thought about Londen and then responded.

"No."

"Do you plan to go to college? Although I hear you really don't need a degree for IT, just certificates."

"That is true but I do plan to go to college. I'm not sure what I want to major in."

"I'm sure you could do just about anything. You look young."

"Is that your way of asking me how old I am?"

"Well I know you're over 25 but not over 40. I give you 32 or 33."

"And women say men play games."

"Oh Patrick, I'm just having some lunchtime fun with

you. A much different me than the lady from the fueling station?"

"You're funny. I've never heard anyone in the United States call a gas station a fueling station."

"Have you traveled abroad?"

"More questions." I laughed.

"Just another bonus if you have."

"I didn't know I was being rated. Yes I have."

She laughed as she placed her fork on her plate. She didn't finish her meal. I placed my fork down as well though I was still hungry. My mind drifted to Maison and Thad. What was I doing here? Why was I wasting this young lady's time? Though I enjoyed sitting here talking to her, I knew Patrick, the guy she thought she was talking to was a wanted man using an alias whose hands had too much blood on them and whose closet was overflowing with skeletons banging on the door. She caught me looking across the table at her and smiled. The return of the waiter interrupted our gazing moment as he asked if there would be anything else.

"Would you like dessert?" I asked.

"No thank you. I have too much work to do this afternoon, I would fall asleep in my office."

"If you could leave the check?" I asked the waiter.

When he pulled our bill out from his waistband Althea reached for the small black leather bind. I kindly intercepted and placed it in front of me.

"Patrick! Please allow me. I owe you for the other night."

"No you don't. You can get the next one."

"Who says there'll be a next one Mister?"

"Will there be?"

She smile and stood up.

"I have to get back to work. Not everybody has free time to reassess their careers." She laughed.

"Thank you for meeting me for lunch. I hope to hear from you again." I said.

When we exited the restaurant, Althea turned and extended her hand. I shook her hand. Her grip was firm and she gave direct eye contact. Before we released each other's hand she asked me "Patrick what are you looking for?" That was a loaded question for someone like me. But I gave her an honest answer.

"Someone who understands my soul and the pain it's been through and that's able to love me unconditionally despite my imperfections."

I saw her eyes widen and a small grin appear on her beautiful face. I hope she understood what I was saying because I didn't need a savior. Instead I needed someone nonjudgmental which was hard to find no matter how honest or dishonest you were.

"Patrick! If you don't have any plans this weekend, let's have dinner and get to know more about each other."

I knew standing here that if things went my way by the weekend my *reassessment* would be complete and I'd be in a nonextradition country.

"That sounds nice. Give me a call and let me know what you have in mind." I said.

"I will do that Patrick."

I stared at her chic walk and her titillating body as she turned and walked up the crowded downtown street. Having lunch with her felt different than any other situationship I'd been in. Though I wasn't truthful with her at all, she made me feel like I could trust her even with her important title. When Althea was out of my view, I turned and headed in the direction of Zad's and to the hotel. My walk wasn't fast but I kept up with the law-abiding citizens on the busy sidewalks. I kept my head low and tried my best not to make eye contact with anyone. With the alluring reward being offered for me, I knew any one of these commoners wouldn't hesitate to pull out their cell phone and dial 911. The dark suit I had on felt better than the God awful orange jumper so I moved briskly hoping to reach my destination. When I reached 7th street I turned the corner and walked towards Los Angeles Street. If I was lucky Zad had my other suit ready. As I approached the building I saw Zad standing outside and an unoccupied black and white patrol car parked out front. He had my suit in his hands and when I got closer I saw him shake his head and motioned one of his hands towards the upper level of the building. I stopped walking and stood two blocks from one of the two people who considered me their son. I looked around to see if any more cops were headed this way. The streets were still busy but no sign of black and whites or unmarked dark sedans. Zad started walking up the block. I walked parallel with him, both of us making direct eye contact but my main concern was the front door of the building. By the time we reached 9th street, I could see two cops wearing dark shades exiting the building and looking around. I saw one of them talk into his radio and within seconds two dark unmarked sedans spun around the corner to join them. Four undercover detectives joined them and I couldn't believe my eyes when I saw Henderson exit one of the sedans. It felt as if a bucket of concrete had been poured around my feet. I literally couldn't move. I heard Zad call my name and tell me to keep moving but I couldn't. My internal rage was boiling hotter than the center core of the sun. I had been betrayed again.

"Lance!" I heard Zad.

I looked over at my old friend and motioned for him to move on. I would have to get the suit some other time or not at all. The last thing I wanted to add to my disgraceful conscientious was Zad being arrested and charged as an accomplice. I turned back to the repelling scene in front of the building where I heard my old friend refer to me as his son. The small group that took the oath to protect and serve was looking in my direction. Henderson confirmed my identity because in a matter of seconds they were in their vehicles headed my direction. I saw Zad make his fastest mad dash but I was still standing in the cement. Zad was squatting down next to a building across the street. I looked over at him and apologized for bringing trouble his way. My old friend placed his right hand across the left side of his chest and bowed his head. Even in this time of wrong doing there he was praying for my safety, more than I can say for the sperm donor laid to rest.

When the squad cars got within 30 yards I sprinted up Los Angeles Street. I heard multiple sirens in the area. One of the detectives yelled at me to stop running. Then I heard bullets ricocheting off of the ground and the buildings around me. I pulled out my 9MM and scanned to see which car was unloading their department issued. It was Henderson solely firing his weapon in my direction. He wasn't concerned about arresting me. He wanted me dead because he knew I'd turn him in as part of a plea deal and he'd die a slow death in prison as a crooked cop. I took aim at the driver first. Two bullets hit the windshield and he swerved causing Henderson to drop his weapon. I pointed my weapon at the passenger side and unloaded five shots. I saw a red coloring splash across the windshield and Henderson's head snap back. The car hit a fire hydrant then crashed into a parked car. The other cars were still coming my way. I stood up and ran up Los Angeles Street. Then I turned down a narrow alley and checked every available door until I found one unlocked. I lunged into the back of a flower shop with my weapon pointed in front of me. I saw a middle aged white woman putting a flower arrangement together. She screamed when she saw my gun and dropped the vase on the ground and glass shattered. I put my left finger over my lips and told her I wasn't there to hurt her or rob her. She covered her face and starting crying. I asked her if anyone else was in the shop. She said in a low crying voice that she was alone. I continued moving slowly to the front of the store. When I got to the front the streets looked normal and I didn't hear any sirens. I stood off to the side looking left then back right for any signs of L.A.'s finest. I had to get back to the hotel and get my vehicle. The lady in the flower shop was still standing in the same spot. Her face was pale and she was shaking. I saw her look at the cell phone on the counter.

"Look I'm not going to hurt you."

"Please Mister just take what you want and get out of my shop."

"Lady I don't want anything from you or your shop. Just give me a minute."

"I won't call the cops. I promise. Please just don't hurt me." She pleaded.

"Not every black man with a gun is out to hurt you."

"Not every white woman thinks that. But you do have a gun and you have been shot. Obviously, you're into some shady dealings."

The adrenaline rush had numbed the pain but my left arm had been grazed by one of Henderson's bullets. It was a flesh wound but the material of my suit coat was ripped. I wouldn't be able to walk the streets without drawing attention to myself.

"Do you have a first aid kit?"

"I thought you didn't want anything from me?"

"Never mind."

"It's in the bathroom behind the vanity. Would like me to get it or are you like most men?"

"How are most men?"

"They're scare of a little pain and cry for their mothers at the first sign of blood."

"You haven't been around men then. Yes please get the first aid kit."

I took my suit coat off and then my shirt and under shirt. When the flower shop owner returned she stopped and the first aid kit hit the floor.

"What's the matter? You never saw a black man half naked?"

She had her hands over her mouth but didn't say anything.

"Lady, will you bring the first aid kit over here? I need to get out of your shop, remember?"

She picked up the small box of medical supplies and walked over slowly towards me.

"You know, I should change the sign on my door to *closed* before a customer walks in."

"That's not necessary. I should be done in no time."

She ignored me and turned her sign around and locked the door. Then she came towards me and turned a key lockbox on the wall and a black store front gate came down from the ceiling. We kept our eyes on each other. When the gate fully deployed she opened the kit and pulled out some gauze, betadine and bandages.

"You've been injured before I see."

"I didn't know I was being examined."

She poured the betadine onto the gauze and applied it to my small wound. It stung a little as she gently dabbed it onto my skin. I heard sirens and jumped.

"Come sit down and relax so I can finish cleaning this."

"When did the hospitality team walk in?" I asked.

"You're such a smart ass."

"You don't know anything about me."

"I know you're in my store with a gun and acting ungrateful." She said.

"I was always taught to say thank you after you receive something."

"Well, closing my shop and letting down a security gate wasn't for my protection."

"Thank you!"

"No you're not so spare me."

I felt her applying the gauze with more pressure now. She opened a large Band Aid and applied it to my flesh wound.

"That should hold you until you can get to safety Lance."

I stood up from the chair and pointed my weapon at the flower shop owner.

"Who did you just call me?"

"I didn't recognize you at first but your face is on every news channel. I put two and two together after a few minutes."

"So why did you help me? Why not call the police?"

"I don't know if you're guilty or innocent and my life is more important than trying to go for a cell phone."

"So you didn't want the reward money just for turning me in?"

"Lance you should get going. Don't worry about me telling the cops anything."

The Good Samaritan told me to go to the back of her shop until she reopened for business. Then it would be easier for me to walk out of the front door instead back through an alley. Her kindness was strange but it was all I had to go on. I put my clothes on and proceeded to the back of her shop and waited for the all clear. My cell phone started buzzing in my pocket. It was Townsend.

"Yeah?" I answered.

"Have you set things in motion yet?"

"No! I had to make a detour."

"Why?"

"An anonymous tip brought the cops to the downtown L.A. shopping district."

"Seriously Lance! You're shopping right now?"

"The jogging suits and khakis were getting old Townsend! I have everything under control."

"Doesn't appear that way to me if you're worried about how you look."

"Like I said I have everything under control. You're free to leave California anytime you get ready."

"Leave? So I can receive a phone call telling me you're dead or back in police custody with your designer suit on?" He laughed.

"Oh so you don't think I have this under control?"

"If you did, Maison and the young cop wouldn't still be breathing."

"You do things your way and I do things my way."

"And how's that working for you?"

"Townsend! Do you have a lead on Catalina?"

He hung up! I knew what button to push to stop his book manual preaching on how to kill a person. The humanitarian inside the flower shop came to the back and told me the coast appeared to be clear.

"What is your name Miss?"

"My name isn't important. Please get out of my stop as quick as you barged in."

I looked at the glass on the floor from our initial meeting. The nameless secret holder gave me a look that told me she'd take care of it. I looked at her one last time before heading to the front of her shop. I wanted to ask her name again but looking at her told me it was pointless. She had cleaned my wound and swore to keep her mouth closed. Enough had been said and it was time to move on. Time to prove I could pull the trigger of an automatic weapon without emotional ties. When I open the door everything seemed normal. You couldn't tell a shootout had taken place; one officer dead from greed and being a colluder, the other in the wrong place at the wrong time. I looked up at the sign above my head – The Tilted Tulip was the name of her shop. As I wandered up Broadway, my paranoid meter was in overload. Every horn made me jump. People were bumping into me and I would stagger. People walking probably thought I was high on something the way I was acting. The perfect disguise to distract them from looking at me for too long and placing my face with the face they'd seen the last time they watched the local news.

As I approached the hotel nothing appeared out of the ordinary. A young freckled face kid was working the valet. I needed to go upstairs and unfortunately change back into a jogging suit. The rip in my jacket would draw attention. I gave the valet attendant my ticket and told him I needed to run up to my room and I would be back in 10 minutes. He took my ticket and unlocked the cabinet to get my keys before running off to the parking lot to get my car. I entered the busy lobby and saw Benji working the hotel front counter. He looked up as I rushed past.

"Good evening Sir."

I didn't return the greeting. I waved and kept moving at a fast pace. When I got to the elevator there was a group of tourists. I heard them speaking German and talking about America's economy and the upcoming election. Some of the things they were saying I agreed with but I wasn't in the mood for a political debate. When the elevator doors opened they stepped inside and gave me a look of disapproval with hopes I would take another lift up.

"Guten Tag!" I said and stepped in and pushed my floor. They didn't say anything during the elevator ride. When the elevator reached their floor they exited quietly. As soon as the doors began to close I heard them chatting about my raggedy suit jacket and my familiar face. I reached my floor and rushed to my room. As much as I hated to admit it, I wouldn't last much longer walking the streets and circulating in common areas. Someone was sure to recognize my face again and make the call for the reward money. I grabbed all of my belongings and took one last look around before I closed the door. I walked out of the elevator on the lobby level and saw the nice hostess from earlier. She smiled at me and I struggled to crack the corners of my mouth but returned a half smile, half smirk. Benji saw me approaching.

"Are we checking out sir?"

I didn't answer him. Instead I gave him a look that told him it really depends.

"Let me know if there's anything we can do to make your stay better." He continued.

I acknowledged his hospitality with a nod and kept moving through the lobby to the valet. I wasn't sure if I would return to the hotel once I left. I couldn't risk those Fritz catching the evening news and placing my face. My car was waiting for me in front of the hotel. The lively attendant approached me to help me with my bags but I bluntly asked him to open the trunk for me. I put what was left of my life in the trunk and looked for another clip to load into my 9MM. I could feel the inquisitive attendant trying to see what I was doing. I stood up from the trunk and gave him a generous tip with an irritated look. He rushed back to the valet stand and didn't look in my direction. After I found the clip, I did my best to slide the semi-automatic weapon under my sweat suit jacket without the valet noticing it. I closed the trunk and walked to the driver's side. Before I got inside I saw a black SUV parked about 50 yards away. I looked around to see if there were any other blacked out SUVs close by but didn't see any. I got inside the Crown Victoria and pulled away from the hotel looking in my rearview mirror to see if the black SUV would follow. I didn't see the SUV pull away from its parked position. I proceeded towards Figueroa Avenue and made a right turn. As I made the turn I looked in my rearview mirror and saw the headlights of the black SUV come on. I remember in high school my driver's training instructor telling me to accelerate through my turns. I did just that and changed lanes quickly trying to reach 8th Street before the driver of the SUV reached Figueroa Avenue. I reached 8th Street and I could hear horns blowing. I saw the black SUV swerving in and out of lanes in pursuit of me. I made the left turn on 8th Street. The 110 Freeway on ramp was a few blocks ahead but traffic was moving at a snail's pace. I was sitting at a red light on Francisco Street. I saw the black SUV turn onto 8th Street but it was stuck in between the intersection and 8th Street. I saw someone exit the passenger side in a dark suit. They were jogging in my direction. He was about 6 ft. 6 in tall and looked Serbian. The light turned green but my rearview mirror visual was only 3 cars back. I saw him pull out a weapon and point it in my direction. Next I heard the familiar popping sound as one of the bullets hit the passenger side of my car. I pressed the gas pedal to the floor and hit the car in front of me. My tires were spinning in place creating a smoke cloud but I could still hear the sound of bullets. Another one hit my car then another hit the back windshield. I returned fire through the shattered glass. I saw the gunmen duck down behind one of the cars. I pushed the car out of my way enough to proceed forward. I couldn't enter the 110 Freeway so I kept up 8th Street as the hired foreigner continued unloading his weapon at me. The black SUV made it through the traffic and the gunmen got back inside. I could see them speeding to fulfill their contract of ending my life. I made a quick right on Garland Avenue near an apartment complex and a hotel. I turned into the apartment complex and jumped out of the damaged Crown Victoria with my semi-automatic in hand. I ran to the driveway opening and leaned against the wall with my weapon positioned to fire. I could hear the SUV's engine. He was nearby. When I saw the front end of the SUV I squeezed the trigger. Bullets sprayed the right side of the vehicle as the vehicle swerved and hit the curb and the horn of the SUV blared mixing in with the local traffic and airplanes overhead. I stayed against the wall to see if anyone would come from the apartments or move inside the vehicle. A few seconds went by then the passenger door swung open and I saw the Serbian attempt to get out. His dark suit was covered in blood and his head was bleeding. He looked around before falling to the ground. His injuries were worse than he was acknowledging. I raised my weapon and took aim, then put him out of his misery. I rushed over to the vehicle and searched his pockets. I found his wallet with a driver's license and a couple of credit cards, a pack of cigarettes and some loose change. I pulled the dead driver from the horn and checked his coat pocket. I found a cell phone, more cigarettes and a business card from the hotel I just left. I couldn't reach his back pocket but I could hear sirens in the background coming closer to my location. I ran back to my vehicle and got back on 8th Street in the direction of the 110 Freeway. I drove the speed limit as a black and white squad car zoomed past me. I kept checking my rear view mirror to see if my car had been reported in the gunfire exchange. The squad car continued westbound in the direction of the deadly crime scene. As I waited at the traffic light to turn onto the 110 Freeway the hotel business card was troubling me. I thought about Benji and if our reunion had been the curse I was afraid of. I knew the cell phone would lead me to who hired the goons.

I turned on the radio and heard the lyrics of a great R&B singer screaming mother, mother and saying war is not the answer. That melody took my mind away for what felt like an eternity before I heard a honking horn because I wasn't driving fast enough. I flipped him the bird before changing lanes. As he zoomed by I gave him a dirty look with my finger resting against my window. I merged onto the 101 Freeway and saw the mileage sign that said Calabasas 23 miles. I pulled out the dead man's cell phone and dialed the last number. A voice answered quickly.

"Is it done?" the voice said.

"No! It's just getting started." I told him.

Silence intruded our phone call.

"Don't get quiet now Maison!" I said.

"I underestimated you Lance."

"I know how that feels. I did the same with you."

"No chance of us forgetting the whole thing?" He

asked.

"Not in this lifetime!"

"You know it's just a matter of time before the cops catch you."

"You'll be dead before that happens."

"Don't be so sure."

"I've never felt more certain Maison."

"Good luck!"

He hung up.

I continued on the 101 Freeway North. I called Townsend but he didn't answer. I didn't leave a message and didn't follow up with a text message. I decided I wouldn't contact Townsend again until I had Maison in my possession. I got into the far right lane to drive at a lesser speed without irritating my fellow Andretti drivers. I turned the volume up on the station playing old school R&B. That era of music cleared my head and got my mind right. Driving to Calabasas I knew I wouldn't be able to nab Maison but I had to see where he slept so soundly. I needed another pawn to aid in my attack. There was only one person that could do that for me – Sydney. I took exit 25A off the 101 Freeway. The city of Woodland Hills was the next door neighbor to Calabasas. I made a left onto Serrania Avenue in search of a hotel or motel to lay my head for the night. I passed several low end stores, some Asian markets and restaurants and a couple of gas stations. No hotels or motels in sight. The cell phone I had unfortunately didn't have the fancy apps to help me with my search. I turned into one of the gas station to get some help. A couple of people were putting gas in their vehicles. I parked my car and walked up to the thick window. The older gentlemen turned away from his small television and asked me if he could help me.

"Sir, can you tell me where the nearest hotel is?"

"If you stay on Serrania Ave a few more blocks, there's a Best Western on the right."

Out of my peripheral vision I saw the breaking news pop up on the mini tube keeping him company. A reporter was live in downtown Los Angeles standing in front of the Tilted Tulip. The old guy stopped talking to me to hear the latest breaking news.

*This is Amanda **Tgyuen** reporting live from downtown L.A. where the manhunt for Lance Goodman may have gotten its first lead since he fled the hospital. Afternoon commuters believe they saw the man wanted for multiple murders walking out of a flower shop earlier today. The flower shop owner has denied seeing the fugitive and has cooperated* *with the authorities as they search her place of business. The city urges citizens to please call the police if they see this man who is considered to be armed and dangerous. Reporting live from Downton Los Angeles this is Amanda Tgyuen.*

When he returned to the thick glass between us I had pulled the bill of my hat down low so you could barely see my eyes and face. He asked me if I needed anything else.

"Yeah! $30 on pump 1."

"Regular or Premium?"

"Regular."

I slid the money under the glass and returned to pump 1. As I pumped the gas I thought about Althea and I could also see the gas station attendant eyeing me. I talked to the pump as if it could hear me and told it to speed up. I finished pumping the gas and got back in my car en route to the recommended hotel. When I got back on Serrania Avenue and glanced in my rearview mirror I could see the old man standing outside of the gas station kiosk looking in my direction. He must have recognized me from the breaking news. I contemplated getting back on the 101 Freeway in the direction of Los Angeles but I needed to rest a bit and I needed to spend some time on the phone trying to convince Sydney to help me. I saw the Best Western sign ahead at the same time I saw a Woodland Hills Sheriff squad car dash past me. As I turned into the parking lot of the hotel I saw the squad car continue past the gas station. I exhaled a momentary breath of relief as I approached the entrance to check the room availability. I kept my cap pulled down low over my face as I entered the lobby. It was empty and quiet inside the low budget tavern and one person was working the front counter. I didn't see a bar or lounging area. There was a small desk off from the front counter with a computer and a printer. Above it there was a sign displayed that said *Business Center.* The walls needed to be repainted and the drab paintings of flowers and old barn houses with skinny horses needed to be replaced.

"Can I help you?" The customer rep rudely asked.

"Good evening!"

She stood there unresponsive.

"Do you have any rooms available?" I asked.

She started typing but didn't ask me if I preferred smoking or non-smoking, king or 2 doubles.

"We have 1 room with a 2 double beds."

She didn't ask me if I wanted it or tell me the price. She stood there with the same unresponsive look chewing gum as she had when I approached the front counter.

"How much is the room per night?"

"Do you need it for more than one night?" The same rudeness present.

"I may."

"It's available for tonight only." I heard her sulk.

"I'll take it. Thanks."

"Credit card and license please."

"I would like to pay cash."

"A $300 deposit is required."

I gave her the deposit and my driver's license and asked if they served breakfast. She started putting my information into the computer and stayed consistent with her rudeness.

"Breakfast is from 6:30 – 9:00 AM."

She handed me the key card inside the small envelope without writing my room number on the outside.

"What room number?" I asked.

"416!"

I didn't waste any more of my kindness on the lifeless person standing before me. I walked away towards a sign indicating where the elevators were located. When I walked into my room I immediately knew I had a smoking room. No matter how much they cleaned and deodorized smoking rooms, the stench of a smoker still lingered. I dropped my bags on the dingy carpet then sat on one of the double beds. The mattress was hard and I saw a couple of cigarette burn holes confirming this was a smoking room. I pulled out my cell phone and dialed Sydney's number, not sure what I was going to ask her but her phone only rang twice before she answered.

"Hello!"

"Hi Sydney, how are you?"

"I'm sorry who's speaking?"

"It's me Sydney." Hoping she'd remember.

"The voice sounds a little familiar but I can't remember."

"You used to work for me."

The silence had its hands around my throat.

"Why are you calling me? We have nothing to talk about."

"I need your help Sydney, please."

"I'm not a lawyer." She screamed.

"I know that but you used to tell me your acting skills were second to none."

"What does my acting have to do with helping you? You're a murderer!"

Her words cut deeper than a 9" chef knife.

"Can we meet me to discuss this?"

"There's nothing to discuss Lance."

"Sydney my life depends on your help. Please I need you."

The silence has come back.

"Ok Lance! Where would you like to meet? And when?"

"Do you remember me telling you my favorite place to go when I first moved to California?"

"I really don't have time for games and riddles Lance. Just tell me!"

"This isn't a game. If you calm down and think for a moment it will come to you."

"Don't tell me to calm down. I'm talking to a murderer."

I needed her so I dealt with her emotional outrage but I also knew how to put things in perspective for her.

"Look Sydney, I'll pay you."

"How much?"

"What do auditions normally pay?"

"This isn't an audition. You said you need me, right?"

"$25,000!"

"I won't take less than $50,000!"

Without knowing what I wanted her to do she had set

her price; a price that could be the death of her.

"So I will see you in the morning at 10 AM?"

"Will you have my money?"

"After we discuss what I need you to do if you're still interested you'll receive half upfront and the rest when you complete the task."

"What if you're captured and in prison?"

"Don't count on that happening?"

"What's your plan B? OJ's attorney is gone!"

"You'll get your money Sydney!"

"Don't snap at me!"

My fists were clenching and my patience was wearing thin. She was the same as she was in the print shop. I said thanks and hung up before I pissed her off and blew the deal. I got up from the bed and walked to the bathroom to take a shower. I didn't even look at my reflection in the mirror. It was evident that I was mentally disturbed and had no concern for anyone's life. Not even my own. The shower tub had a small bug crawling around the water sprout and I could see a visible dirt ring. I guess housekeeping didn't make it to this item on the cleaning checklist. When I turned on the water the bug scurried down the side unto the bathroom floor. I didn't kill him and he kept moving quickly into a small crack in the wall under the sink. I waited for the water to reach its maximum temperature. I stuck my hand inside after a few minutes and I was surprised to feel the burning hot water. I quickly undressed and jumped in the shower. I used the complimentary bar of bath soap and one of the face cloths to wash up. When the hot water splashed against my flesh wound it hurt like hell. Just as I began to wash my legs I could feel the water temps getting weak so I rushed to finish before it turned ice cold. I stepped out of the shower and my bathroom guest was back crawling around. I ignored his world of freedom and finished getting dressed. That little guy was freer than I'd ever be.

I powered up one of my laptops to see how much Maison has used his credit card. The account I had set up had $100,000 in it illegally transferred from his credit card. By the time his billing statement came out he'd be dead and his estate planner would have the task of finding the transfers. I looked at his website to see what properties he had available and reasonably priced. I grabbed my cell phone and called Townsend. I was going to make it quick and to the point. I wasn't up for his inquiries. The phone began to ring and I immediately felt shaky. Townsend picked up on the second ring.

"If it isn't Mr. GQ?"

"I need a female business profile made quickly!"

"For whom? For what?"

"Can you get it or not?"

"Calm down GQ."

"Cut that shit out and answer the question."

"Okay I'll get it for you. How old do you want her to be?"

"Early 30's."

"What's the business platform?"

"Real estate investor for architectural engineering firms."

"You going all out I see."

"Maison came after me today. With my face airing around the clock on every local channel I'm not going to be able to grab him on my own."

"And you think a female real estate investor can help you?" he laughed.

"Man's biggest weakness is a pair of heels! You told me that remember?"

"Well played. Okay I'll have the profile up and live by morning."

"Thanks!"

"Glad to see you back on track."

I wanted to ask him so bad about Catalina. I hung up.

Instead I kept looking at Maison's website. He had two locations that most likely would get his interest. Both properties had been on the market close to a year. One was in downtown Los Angeles and the other was on Wilshire Boulevard not too far from my old therapist. I closed the laptop and turned on the television to catch some sports or an episode of private islands for sale. Most of the television channels were saturated with commercials about the upcoming elections from the two candidates. Other channels were airing infomercials, shopping hour or the latest reality show. I finally found the sports channel network. Listening to the analysts talk about the baseball playoff picture. I miss going to a ballpark to watch a good baseball game. I thought about how uninterested my sperm donor was in teaching me the sports I grew up loving. I can only remember him lying to me about why he didn't sign me up for the park leagues. He was too busy getting high. My mother would throw the ball with me. She would never throw the ball hard but she did her best. The cell phone buzzing interrupted my childhood memories. It was Althea.

"Hi!"

"Good evening Patrick. Did I disturb you?"

I looked around the room filled with a killer's arsenal before answering.

"No you didn't. How are you?"

"I'm doing well. I thought about you and wanted to call."

"How was the rest of your afternoon?"

"It was insanely busy. Two police officers were killed and they still haven't caught the murder suspect that escaped from the hospital."

"All that happened after we had lunch?"

"Yes. You didn't hear the gunfire?" She asked.

"No! I left the downtown area after we met. I had some business in Woodland Hills."

"Oh okay. Working on that reassessment I see."

"Yes I am."

"Are you sure Friday isn't a problem. I felt weird after suggesting it. That's not me normally." She said.

"Yes I'm looking forward to it. Where would you like to meet?"

"I like the Santa Monica area. Is that fine?"

"Works for me."

"I picked the restaurant last time so you pick this time."

"Okay I will let you know by Friday."

"Casual dress okay?"

This conversation was sounding like a real date in a

relationship. My conversations in the past couple of years basically were about my location, how much time and if I wanted anything special. Althea was playing with my mind and didn't even know it. She was about to walk the public streets with a wanted murderer.

"Yes I'm wearing jeans and a casual shirt."

Damn that just rolled off my tongue like I was still in Los Feliz Hills with a closet full of clothes living a normal life.

"Okay Patrick. See you on Friday and feel free to call or text before then."

"Talk to you soon."

I was a fugitive on the run trying to kill the bastard who set me up and starting a situationship with someone who would have no choice but to turn me in once she found out who I really was. I lay on the hard double bed thinking of everything I needed to tell Sydney in the morning. This was a one time shot at capturing Maison. I'm sure he's replaced the dead hit men from this morning. The next crew will be much tougher. Neither one of us would rest until the other was dead. Men like Maison didn't care about reward money. After I meet with Sydney I will head to Gardena to see if Thad has been around the old gun range. Then drive by his neighborhood and plan his untimely death before his hearing. In the midst of all this I have to find a pair of jeans, shirt and something besides these sneakers I've been wearing. No way I could go back to the shopping district. My luck was running out and I didn't have the best spiritual relationship to ask a higher being to watch over me. That's the thing with the devil he's not your savior. Once he has you in his grasp you can't stop doing the devil's work. He convinces you that greed is the best way. Just this one time becomes another time and then the blood trail never ends.

It was close to midnight when my cell phone started buzzing non-stop from an unknown number. I didn't answer the first few times and then it just become annoying.

"What?"

"You're still free?"

"You knew that before you called. What do you want Maison?"

"What do you say I tell you where your immigrant housekeeper is and we call it even."

"You know where Catalina is?"

"Maybe."

"Playing games will only make me torture you more before I finally kill you."

"Even as a fugitive, your arrogance still amazes me."

"It's not arrogance. Do you know where Catalina is or not?"

"What is it about that old lady?

"This is my last time asking."

He hung up. Now I couldn't sleep. Townsend wouldn't tell me if he knew where Catalina was. Maison was making propositions of a truce in exchange of her whereabouts. My head was spinning fast and I developed a migraine. I went to the window and looked out into the night. The quiet of the night gave you calmness and some clarity or it confused you more and clouded your judgment. I could see Sydney's young face and her smile in the night air. She hadn't even begun to live her life. She hadn't even started acting and hadn't even had a boyfriend because she was so serious about her career. Maison would surely kill her if he suspected foul play and found out she was connected to me. Thinking about all of that I felt my eyes starting to burn. I blinked quickly a few times and it happened just like that. A tear ran down the left side of my face and then another tear fell from the right eye. I wiped my face and went to the bathroom and wet my face with cold water trying my best not to look at my reflection in the mirror. I knew one glimpse of my devilish cheekbones and conniving eyes and

I wouldn't give a damn about some fame chasing broad and I'd just as well see her dead like all the others. I dried my face and noticed my bathroom companion was roaming the bathroom floor free without a care in the world other than a bright light coming on and someone killing him before we could make it back to the small crack in the wall. Stay as long as you like my friend.

I sat on the side of the double bed and looked at all of my belongings on the other bed; then at the cell phone on the wooden nightstand. I took in the décor of the room and thought of how I would tell Sydney I had changed my mind. I picked up the cell phone and scrolled to her number but my finger wouldn't press the button to connect the call. I sat holding the phone in my hand long enough for the screen to reset back to the home screen but it felt like an eternity. Again I went to recent calls and scrolled to her number and my finger hovered over the button to connect the call. The devil had his arms around my soul squeezing every ounce of good out of me. His pitchfork was stabbing me repeatedly in my heart. He was putting his final spell on me so I'd be left running on empty; leaving nothing for myself to go on living. I sat the cell phone back on the nightstand and lay across the bed. The digital clock displayed 1:05 AM as I closed my eyes.

It was 5:22 AM when I woke up. My body was a little stiff from the uncomfortable bed. I lifted my arm and felt pain from my wound. I looked at the cell phone and I had two text messages from Townsend giving me the information for the business profile, bank accounts and past clients. I sent him a text message expressing my gratitude. He replied right back with not exactly the same sentiments – *handle your business Lance.*

I didn't reply and started getting dressed. I went downstairs for breakfast. The small lobby was much different than the Miyuki hotel. There was an older couple sitting having coffee and toast. They had on Hawaiian looking shirts and matching shorts. The small area was a self-serve set up with cereal, two types of milk, a carafe of cranberry juice and a toaster. The white and wheat bread was on the side of the toaster with a small bowl of butter and assorted jellys. I saw a stainless steel canister with coffee and some sugar, sweeteners and cream. I didn't see any tea bags or a hostess to ask. When my toast was done I grabbed a cup of juice and headed to a small table. I made eye contact with the older man and nodded. He returned the gentlemen's nod. He and his lady companion looked like retirees traveling to all of the states in the union by a recreation vehicle.

"Young man would you like to see the newspaper? I'm finished with it."

"Sure sir. Thank you."

He stood up and as he approached his frail pail legs showed he'd earned his right to move at his own pace. He and the lady sitting with him were probably proud parents and grandparents. Maybe even great grandparents.

"Here you go sonny. I sure hope they catch that murderer soon. He's all over the news."

There I was on the front page of the local newspaper. Good thing his eyes weren't that good because he would have gone into cardiac arrest had he known he was having breakfast with the face on the front page.

"I'm sure L.A.s finest will catch him soon. Thanks for the paper."

"You're welcome sonny. Have a good day."

His lady companion stood up when he got back to the table. They interlocked fingers and slowly walked out of the hotel. I sat there and enjoyed the continental breakfast and read all about myself on the front page and page 2A. The article talked about my birthplace of North Carolina, my military career, the print shop being nothing but a front for criminal activity and my possible whereabouts. It went on to say I once held an account at the local bank downtown. Jordan and the branch manager's name were mentioned. If I had to say so myself the article was thorough with a few details missing. I laughed to myself and folded the paper up and finished my coffee before heading back upstairs.

I gathered up my gear in the room and returned to the front desk to get the balance of my cash deposit. There was an older lady working this morning. She greeted me when I approached the counter and I returned the greeting.

"Was everything good with your stay sir?"

"Yes, thank you."

"Are we checking out?"

"Yes please."

"Room number?"

"416."

"I see you paid cash. Let me get your change and your receipt."

She counted out my change and handed me a receipt. I thanked her and left the hotel. The morning temperature felt like it was in the 80s already. I put my gear in the trunk and kept a loaded 9MM with me. When I started up the Crown Victoria I sat there while the engine warmed up and I saw Sydney's face and smile again. My eyes didn't burn this morning and unconscientiously I looked in the rearview mirror. In the corner of it was the devil leaning with his arms folded. He spoke to my soul and convinced me that Sydney was disposable like all the others; the sacrifice of a meaningless being for my greater good. Use her Lance and let her fend for herself he told me. After receiving confirmation I put the automatic transmission in reverse and headed towards the 101 Freeway South ready to pay the $25,000 deposit.

The morning traffic was heavy as most drivers were heading to downtown L.A. for work. I turned the radio to the sports talk channel and flowed with the traffic. I felt safe driving in traffic because everybody was busy drinking their morning brew, putting on makeup, texting or talking on the phone, and changing in and out of lanes. My cell phone started buzzing. I looked at the screen and it displayed a 213 area code number. I let it ring a few more times before I answered.

"Hello!"

"Good morning Sir. It's Benji. I was calling to see if you were checking out this morning?"

"Hi Benji. No I won't be."

"Great! Let us know if we can do anything to improve your stay."

"Everything is fine."

"Have a good day Sir."

"Benji!"

"Yes Sir."

"Have I had any visitors?"

"No Sir. It's been quiet. I can ask my colleagues. One moment."

When he returned to the line he told me no one had inquired about me. I extended my gratitude and hung up. I was approaching the 405 Freeway southbound interchange. Traffic was flowing better southbound. As I approached the Wilshire Boulevard exit I began to get nervous and was having second thoughts. I wondered if I had a daughter how would I have raised her? Would I have had an impact on her life to be able to see through men and not be used? Would I have provided a stable upbringing for her to support her dreams? Why hadn't Sydney's father done that for her? Why was she willing to accept money from an accused murderer? From any man! My sentimental thoughts drove me past the Wilshire Boulevard exit. As soon as I looked in the rearview mirror that image of the devil was ever present and immediately tormented my soul and reminded me of Maison, past killings and told me no one loved me not even my own mother and father. He didn't stop tormenting me until my tight grip around the steering wheel changed lanes to take the next exit. He stayed in the corner of the rearview mirror until I made it back to Wilshire Boulevard. Before he disappeared he made sure I understood what needed to be done by asking me what did my mental freedom mean to me? Sydney was an instrumental piece of that. The evil in me wanted revenge but that didn't necessarily mean I'd be mentally free. I needed an ocean of holy water and fleet of angels around me. But the devil was the best at convincing your mind otherwise.

When I got close to La Brea Tar Pits my mind was in a careless state and the sooner Sydney could convince Maison she was a legitimate business woman, the sooner I could get on to the next chapter of my life. Hopefully Sydney would get a chance to enjoy her money but that wasn't my concern this morning. I came to the tar pits shortly after I moved to the Los Angeles area because I was fascinated with dinosaurs growing up. Other than a few small exhibits in the museums in North Carolina I had never seen anything like this and it amazed me from the first time I visited. The way the museum staff kept up the dinosaurs and fossil exhibits was truly a sight to see. A lot had changed since then and I wasn't interested in the exhibits today. I parked my vehicle with the missing back window and grabbed another clip before walking towards the entrance. I didn't see Sydney when I got close to the entrance. A few large groups were forming in the ticket line so I stood off to the side to wait for her. I checked the clock on my cell phone – 10:07 AM and no sign of Sydney. I looked around to see if someone else was coming in her place, the police perhaps. After all the reward money required a phone call and my whereabouts versus her having no idea what I wanted her to do for $50,000. I saw two police officers approaching the entrance gates. One of the officers looked my way. My hat was pulled down but our eyes made contact. He extended a gentlemen's nod and I returned the courtesy. He and his partner continued to the entrance. They stopped at one of the windows then proceeded into the attraction. A few minutes went by then I saw Sydney walking towards me. She had on a pair of dark fitting jeans, a lightweight brown woven sweater and a pair of ankle boots with a small heel. Her caramel skin tone was still young and flawless. Her lips were full and glossy. Her hair was pulled back in a bun and she had a satchel bag across her left shoulder. Her tiny frame hadn't changed at all. She was on her cell phone, hopefully not confirming me being here. She finished up just before walking up to me. She folded her arms as soon as she put her cell phone away and was chewing gum.

"So what's up Lance?"

I immediately looked around to see if anyone heard her. Everyone was busy getting their tickets in line.

"No names please. Good morning."

"Whatever!"

Her attitude was evident.

"Look you don't have to do this."

"I'm here aren't I?"

"Yes with major attitude."

"Listen are you going to tell me what you need or not?"

Before I answered I looked at her. She was young, thriving, in search of stardom and childless. An honest person from what I remembered about her. Last I knew she hadn't sold her soul to the industry under false promise if she slept with someone she'd grace the big screen. There wasn't a big difference between the Hollywood predators and me. One waved the "big" chance in your face after you did something out of your character; the other standing here was waving a monetary enticement with much more risk - death. I felt that old smirk forming on my face and I told the young actress yes and told her let's go into the museum. I told her we'd walk around for a little while then find a sitting area. Walking through the museum I couldn't help but take pleasure in being back there. Sydney and I spoke infrequently along the walk. I could see Sydney was clearly uninterested in the prehistoric artifacts and she kept pulling her cell phone out checking it and responding to text messages or emails. After all we weren't on a date but I hope she'd paid attention when we discussed the details of her acting role. One slip up wouldn't mean a director's cut and retake. It could mean her life most likely. She pointed out an empty bench next to the Stegosaurus. We sat down and a group of middle school kids stood next to us discussing the Stegosaurus and its history. Listening to all of their loaded questions for the tour guide that feeling of emptiness crept up inside me. I would never have a kid asking me questions like these young scholars were asking the tour guide. Then I looked at Sydney and thought the same thing about her as we began to discuss her mission.

"So here's the deal. I need to pose as a business woman interested in purchasing some commercial real estate."

"That's it?" She asked.

"Yes but there's more to it."

"Like what?"

"I need you to make the owner fall for you."

"What do you mean?" She almost said my name.

"I mean come across professional but flirt."

"How far does this flirting need to go?"

"Have you ever flirted with anyone?"

"Yes!"

"Then you know how far it needs to go."

"And the business part?"

"He needs to believe without a doubt you're for real."

"I don't know." She almost said my name again.

"You will have time to prepare. I've set up a business profile for you to memorize."

"Hmmm. So there's no real script?"

"No I'm afraid not."

"And where do you fit in all of this?"

"When you get close to sealing the deal, I'll tell you."

"Why can't you tell me now?"

"Are you still interested?"

"I don't know now."

"Receive half today and the balance when you seal the deal."

I didn't say anything else and looked away at the exhibits. Her hesitance was probably in her best interest and I couldn't appear desperate. She would make a counter offer on the $50,000 if I showed weakness. I could see her looking at her nails and biting her bottom lip then looking around the museum. I could tell she was battling with the decision. I stood up and began to walk away towards one of the exhibits. She must have thought I was leaving.

"Wait!"

I stopped but didn't turn around. She called for me to come back to the bench without saying my name. I kept my back turned to her and didn't move.

"Please!"

What desperate state had Sydney gotten herself into that she was now pleading for me to return to the bench? When I turned around I saw Sydney bent over with her head in her hands. The sight of her infuriated the devil inside me because he knew if I thought about her feelings long enough I would walk away from the deal just like I drove past the exit ramp the first time. I heard the voice of Maison telling me *Good luck* and walked towards the bench with one thing in mind; give Sydney his name, where his business is and the location of the property along with half of her money. When I got back to the bench I didn't get a chance to say anything.

"Did you do the things they're saying you did?"

"No!"

"Why don't you turn yourself in then?"

"I need you to do this one thing before I can prove my innocence."

"Do you have an attorney?"

"Yes I have a legal team."

"And they're advising you to take this route?"

The inquisition was becoming irritating.

"They're paid to do what I tell them."

"I think there's a better way." She almost said my name again.

"Well I've always done things my own way. Are you interested?"

She looked off and didn't answer.

"What if someone recognized you and saw me talking to you?"

"I'd tell them we just started up a conversation here at the museum."

"Yeah but we met outside."

"If someone saw us talking and recognized me, the police would have been here by now."

She was biting her bottom lip again.

"Okay I'll do it."

Just like that her hands outstretched in front of me for half of the payment. It's been said the devil has millions of souls at his disposal. Sydney had demons of her own. The devil had no favorites. We were all used for his greater goal of total reign over mind body and soul. I looked around to see if it was safe to pull out her money. Thirty feet or so away was a small group of kids looking at the Tyrannosaurus Rex. I went into the small backpack and pulled out Sydney's risk of death money. She didn't bother counting it and quickly put the money inside her satchel. She input Maison's information as well as her business profile information in her cell phone and stood up to walk away. She told me she'd be in touch and didn't look back as she headed to the exit of the museum. I sat there for a few minutes before I left thinking to myself the likelihood of this really working or had I just added another innocent soul to my pathetic conscientious.

I made it to the exit and saw the clouds had wrapped their arms around the blue skies from earlier. I walked to my car looking back over my shoulder frequently to see if Sydney had taken half of the money as well as made the phone call to collect the reward money. I didn't see cops coming after me nor did I hear any sirens or see a police chopper circling the area. I did however see two black sedans with black tint on the windows. I slowed my pace to see if I could make out if the license plates were City Government or Federal Government issued. The traffic on

Wilshire prevented my ears from hearing if the engines were running or not. I couldn't see into the front seat or make out how many people were inside each vehicle. I reached the Crown Victoria and they hadn't moved from their parking spaces. As I got into driver's side I pulled the 9MM from the small of my back and placed it in between my legs. I didn't take my eyes off of the two sedans as I started my car. I waited for a break in traffic to enter the westbound traffic on Wilshire Boulevard. I pulled out and kept my eyes on the two cars and as I crossed Crescent Heights Boulevard I saw them pull out. I didn't tell Sydney the place we were meeting. Either I picked up a tail on my way or someone followed Sydney. I could see the two sedans changing in and out of lanes gaining on me. I chambered a round in the 9MM and held it in my right hand and drove with my left hand. They were three cars back in the left lane but I still couldn't make out the driver or the passenger. The traffic light on San Vincente Boulevard turned red but I didn't stop. I heard screeching brakes and horns behind me as the two sedans maneuvered through the heavy intersection of traffic breaking the law just as I had. I sped up a little looking around for a side street to turn down. On the left of me were commercial businesses and on the right a few businesses but more residential homes. I was 4 or 5 miles from the 405 Freeway. The sedans weren't too far away now. I saw a few pedestrians walking on Wilshire Boulevard and traffic wasn't heavy. Then it happened. I heard two or three bullets hit the Crown Victoria. I looked in the rearview mirror and saw a dark-skinned male leaning out of driver's side passenger window of the first car firing an automatic rifle and a fair skin male on the passenger side aiming in my directions. It was Thad! He had Sydney's phone tapped and followed her to La Brea Tar Pits. I made a quick right turn into one of the neighborhoods and floored the bullet filled sedan. I hadn't been hit yet but I was outnumbered so I needed to lose them quickly. I glanced behind me and saw the sedan with Thad in the passenger seat make the same turn I did but I didn't see the other sedan. I made a left turn on the first street I could. They sped down the narrow street still firing in my direction. The Crown Victoria taking more hits and I felt a bullet pierce my right side. I could see a four way intersection ahead as my vehicle continued to receive bullets. I grabbed the steering wheel and turned it sharply to the left and slammed on the brakes. I was facing the oncoming assassins now. I aimed my 9MM at the driver and squeezed the trigger until he lost control of the vehicle and crashed into a parked car. I ran to my trunk and grabbed my automatic rifle to even the playing field. I saw Thad and the dark-skinned shooter get out and kneel down behind the crashed car.

"Lance! Give up, you're outnumbered."

I fired in the direction of the gullible voice trying to convince me this was my fate. I had nothing to say to this ungrateful bastard. They returned fire as I got back in the Crown Victoria. I got in and floored it to the intersection. I saw Thad stand up and talk into a hand held radio before I turned back onto Wilshire Boulevard. I had to make it to the 405 Freeway if I had any chance of them not killing me. I felt the blood on my right side now. My cell phone buzzed. It was Althea – damn.

"Hey!"

"How's it going? Are you busy?"

"Actually, I am in the middle of something. Can I call you back?"

"Sure no problem. Are we still on for this evening?"

Damn it. I'm bleeding now and still don't have a pair of jeans and shirt.

"Yes!"

"Where? You were going to pick remember?"

I heard rubber burning, horns blaring and brakes screeching. Thad was in the other sedan coming for me.

"Ahhh. I will text you the location. I really need to go though. Sorry."

"Are you sure you're okay?"

"Yes! Just trying to finish up something before we meet later."

"Okay see you soon."

I didn't say goodbye and threw the cell phone on the passenger seat. The 405 Freeway was three blocks up ahead. I knew Thad wouldn't open fire on the highway. I needed to decide which direction I was headed. I needed Townsend.

"What's up Lance?"

"Townsend, where are you?"

"I'm by Exposition Park. Why do you sound in a panic?"

"I just got into a shootout with Thad. I need a new car and some back up."

"The young cop shot at you?"

"Yes! I'll catch you up when I see you."

"Where are you right now?" He asked.

"I'm on Wilshire Boulevard, not too far from the 405 Freeway."

"Head southbound and take the Florence Avenue and Manchester Boulevard exit and I'll be there waiting."

"What if I can't make it that far?" I asked.

"You wouldn't have called me if you didn't think you could make it."

He hung up. I looked in my rearview mirror and saw Thad and his crew changing lanes getting closer to me. I floored the Crown Victoria desperately trying to make it to the 405 Freeway. I thought about swerving around the car in front of me to run the yellow caution light but I noticed a black and white squad car at the traffic light waiting to proceed northbound. I could see the on ramp just ahead to the 405 Freeway. When the light turned green I drove fast enough to pass the car in the right lane. Thad and his crew were very close now. The southbound on ramp was busy so I broke the law and rushed through the carpool lane and didn't stop for the red light. The pursuers did the same and didn't slow their speed. Traffic on the 405 Freeway was moving very slow but the carpool lane was wide open. I maneuvered into the carpool again and drove 75 MPH. One quick glance and I saw the black sedan in the same lane. I could really feel the pain of my injury increasing now. What was I going to do about my date with Althea? Townsend called me back and asked if I was on the freeway yet. I told him I was and I still had a tail. He told me not to detour from the Freeway until I reached the exit he told me to take and that everything should be in place by the time I got there. I expressed my appreciation but told him I wanted to be the one to kill Thad. He laughed and told me unless he has a nametag on, X marks the spot for all in pursuit. Beggars couldn't be choosey but I really needed to be the one who kills Thad. I knew Townsend would remind me of how I couldn't handle my business. As I continue on the 405 Freeway those thoughts kept dancing in my head. The exit Townsend told me to take was 3 exits away. I changed lanes and exited the carpool lane. I was in the middle lane now as I approached the airport area. I hadn't been on this side of town in a long time and I was trying to remember the area.

I saw the black sedan still in pursuit and the exit numbers were declining. Without a second thought I took exit 48 La Tijera Boulevard. As I approached the traffic light I saw one of Thad's men lean out of the passenger side window and fire at me. There were 2 other cars at the intersection waiting for the light to turn green. It was now or never. I put the Crown Victoria in park and hopped out and rushed to the trunk to get one of the rifles. Bullets were still coming my way and I heard the tires of the two other cars burn rubber leaving the scene. I obtained a rifle from the trunk as bullets ricocheted off of the pavement. I ran to the front of my vehicle and aimed my rifle in the direction of oncoming traffic. I squeezed the trigger and bullets hit the front windshield but the driver was still coming at me full speed. I continued firing my weapon hitting the hood and one of the front tires. The car chasing me swerved and flipped 2 times. I sprinted to the car with my rifle still aimed at whatever I saw moving. I saw one of the men from the back seat climbing out. I fired two shots to his head and his body went limp onto the roof of the car. I continued moving towards the car and smelt the gas leaking. I didn't have much time. As I got closer I saw the driver was dead and Thad was in the passenger seat unconscious.

I dragged him out of the car. I held the 9MM up to him. The barrel was against his forehead. He gulped hard. I stood back a few feet and shot him in his leg. He screamed out then I shot him in his left shoulder. I could hear sirens in the distance and the ongoing traffic on the 405 Freeway. Thad cursed at me and told me I'd rot in hell. That was the only thing he got right about me. Then I aimed and fired one round to his head. Thad's eyes remained open as his head slumped over. Thad was dead, one to go.

I made it back to my vehicle as I heard sirens getting closer. I took the streets and headed to the city of

Hawthorne. I had two hours before I was supposed to meet Althea. In Hawthorne there were a few shops near the old mall that sold decent clothes. I had to ditch the car as soon as possible. I refuse to call Townsend though. I could hear 2 helicopters flying in the area. I parked the car on 136th Street and checked into a low budget motel on Hawthorne Boulevard. I put all of my belongings in my room and headed back out to buy some clothes. Townsend called and texted me at least a dozen times. I couldn't talk to him right now.

The boulevard was empty and a few shops were starting to close down. I kept walking until I saw a shop that had jeans, urban sweaters and bright suits hanging in the window. I walked in and an Armenian guy asked if I needed any help. I walked around gingerly as the pain was at an all-time high. I grabbed a few pairs of jeans and sport shirts along with a brown casual shoe and a black and brown reversible belt. I paid cash and headed back to the motel. I showered quickly and called for an Uber. I sent Althea a text message and told her to meet me at the 3rd street Promenade in front of Starbucks. My cell phone was buzzing out of control with calls and text messages from Townsend. I didn't answer or reply. He told me to handle my business so that's what I was doing. The Uber app said my driver was 2 minutes away. I looked around my room before heading downstairs. All I had to my life was in this low budget room. I closed the door and jiggled the handle to make sure it was closed and locked.

As the Uber driver pulled up Althea was calling me.

"Hi Althea!"

"How's it going Patrick? I got your text message. Where are we having dinner?"

"I thought we'd meet and take it from there."

"Sounds good. I'm dressed casually."

"So am I."

"See you soon."

I sat in the backseat of my Uber ride and breathed a sigh of relief for the free moments alone I had. I was in a little pain. The Uber driver pulled up in front of the trendy coffee shop and I exited like I was a law abiding citizen. When I closed the car door I immediately saw so many police in the area I started to get back in the car before he pulled off.

"Hi Patrick!"

Too late my date was here already.

"I didn't picture you an Uber man."

"It's convenient for this area without the hassle of parking."

"That's true. I got lucky and caught someone leaving a parking spot in one of the parking garages. Where are we going from here?"

"I thought we'd walk around a bit and grab some sushi."

"That sounds good Patrick."

I couldn't remember the last time I had been on a real date. I reached for Althea's hand and she allowed my fingers to interlock with hers. Then we blended in with the other couples, tourists and locals. I walked slower than normal because my side was killing me. I glanced over at Althea. She had on a pair of jeans, a sweater and some heels. She had a light glossy lipstick on her lips. I saw a white gold ring on her opposite hand and a toggle bracelet.

"So how was the rest of your week after we met?" I asked.

"It was busy. What about you?"

"I'm one step closer to my reassessment being complete."

"That's really good Patrick."

"Thanks!"

When I looked at her I wish I didn't have to lie. As we walked down 3rd street holding hands it just felt right. A few feet in front of us I saw two cops walking towards us. I hadn't noticed but my grip had tightened around Althea's hand.

"Patrick is everything ok?"

I was concentrating on the cops so much that she startled me.

"Yes! Why do you ask?"

"You're holding my hand so tight."

I looked at our fingers interlocked and my hand was gripped to hers like a pair of vise grips. I quickly released her fingers to let the blood circulation return.

"I apologize."

"It's okay. What happen?"

"Oh nothing. I thought I saw on old business associate."

"Things obviously didn't go well because your grip told it all."

"No it didn't end well."

Talking to Althea came easy. So did the lies. By the time we reached the sushi restaurant I could feel myself sweating a little bit from the risk I was taking being in public. The last time I ate at Sugarfish by Sushi Nozawa it was cozy and didn't have TVs hanging everywhere. The restaurant wasn't crowded but we still had to wait to be seated. While we waited to be seated my mind wandered off to thoughts of Sydney and if she'd made contact with Maison. Had she called the police and told them she saw me? Would I ever hear from again now that she has half of the money? Althea brought me back to my present environment.

"I've never been here. Is the sushi good?" She asked.

"It's some of the best in the area."

"Are you a foodie Patrick?"

"What's the point of spending your money on a distasteful meal?" I said.

"I agree. Do you eat fast food?"

"Rarely!"

"Me too but McDonald's fries are the devil."

I laughed thinking to myself *you're standing with one of the devil's most loyal followers.*

"We have something in common." I said.

I heard our party's name called for two. Althea led the way to our table. Her presence was sexy not arrogant and she captured the room's attention with her walk and pleasant smile. When we reached the table she pointed at the chairs and asked if I had to face the door? I laughed and told her she could sit facing the door. We received the paper menus with small pencils and the waiter asked what we'd like to drink. Althea ordered a club soda and I ordered the Ryo Saki. I gazed over at Althea and took in her beauty and thought of our possibilities while looking over the menu. She reminded me of Londen in many ways. She broke my stare and asked if I was ready to order.

"Yes! What are you ordering?" I asked.

"I'm going to order the Trust me."

"I've had that before." I said.

"The menu item or trust itself?" She laughed.

"Both!"

"How was it?" She asked.

"Food was great. The other was disappointing."

"I know how that is. But let's talk about the future not the past. So you said you were close to finishing up your reassessment? That's great Patrick."

"Thank you!"

The waiter was back with our drinks and asked if we were ready to order. Before we could order Althea's cell phone rang. She looked at her phone and silenced it. Who was calling her? An old lover? Someone she's dating? I'm normally not a jealous person but it bothered me. She handed the waiter back the menu and he confirmed her selection of Trust Me. I ordered the same and another glass of Ryo Saki. Then I sat there quietly looking around the restaurant and not at Althea. I've never been good at hiding my facial expressions. She picked up on it.

"Is everything okay Patrick?"

Before I could answer, her cell phone started ringing again. Now I was really annoyed and wanted to get the waiter's attention to change our orders to go. Again she looked at her phone and silenced it. She didn't offer an apology or explanation but asked if I was okay again. I smiled before answering.

"Yes I'm fine. I should be asking if you're okay?" My eyes in the direction of her cell phone.

"Yes I'm fine."

She smiled and outstretched her hands over the table. I hadn't experienced this much affection in years and it felt weird. I extended my hands to touch hers and she looked at the palm of my hands. She rubbed my palms and said they felt strong but soft and that I hadn't done any hard work. I laughed and told her some days were harder than others.

"Patrick are you going to give me a hint on your new career move or remain secretive?"

"I'll tell you when it's finalized."

"That's fair."

"I don't like spilling the beans too soon if you know what I mean."

"My father was the same way. He'd surprised my

mother all the time."

"How would she handle the surprise?"

"She would get upset at some of the things he did without her knowing. But for the most part my parents never argued, at least not in front of us."

"Us? How many siblings do you have?"

"I have a brother two years younger than me."

"Are you guys close?"

"Yes we are. Every year we go someplace together to celebrate our birthday. We were born in the same month."

"What month is that?"

Her cell phone started ringing again.

"One second Patrick."

Hello! Yes this is she. Oh my God! What? When? Any witnesses? This is terrible. Thank you and I'll follow up Monday when I get back in the office.

She finished the call and placed her cell phone on the table. Then Althea lowered her head into her hands for a few minutes. I looked around the restaurant to see if anyone was staring at us. No one was. Good old selfish L.A. I saw her lifting her head and I reached out for her hand. She slowly let it touch mine.

"I'm sorry Patrick. I just received some terrible news."

"It's okay. Are you going to be alright? Do you want to leave?"

"No! I've been looking forward to our date. I will be ok. Excuse me, I just need to go to the ladies room."

"Sure. I'll be right here.

Althea excused herself to the ladies room and I sat there smiling inside. I wasn't sure exactly what was said but it had to do with the death of Thad. She was the district prosecutor for his upcoming trial and that phone call was a devastating blow to the city's case. The way I look at it I did her a favor. She returned to the table just as our food was arriving. As she walked by she softly touched my hand and smiled before sitting down.

"Again I'm sorry Patrick. Our birthdays are in October."

"It's okay really. Can I ask you though, was that a personal or business call?"

"It was a business call that freed up my calendar."

"Is that a good or bad thing."

"Let's eat!" she said.

Her polite way of saying she didn't want to talk about it anymore. I saw her bough her head in prayer like she did at lunch. When she was finished she made the cross across her chest again. My head was lowered but I wasn't praying. I was smiling inside thinking about how I left Thad lifeless on La Tijera Boulevard without any help from Townsend. The old me was back and it scared me.

We ate in silence for the first few minutes. Althea looked everywhere but at me. When the waiter came by our table she ordered some of the Ryo Sake. After he left she sat her chop sticks down and exhaled.

"Are you done?" I asked.

"No! I'm just thinking about that phone call I received."

"That bad?"

"Have you been watching the news?" She asked.

I wasn't sure how to answer the question. One thing I did know. I was a wanted man hanging out in public with a district prosecutor.

"Yes I've caught it here and there."

"Well the cop that was mixed up in a kidnapping case and connected to Lance Goodman, the wanted man for murder was gunned down earlier today. I was working on his case."

"Oh I'm sorry to hear that."

"He was so young. His attorneys had said he wanted to give all the information he had on this Lance Goodman person in exchange for 1 year probation and 6 months house arrest."

"What happens now?" I asked.

"The case will be closed. The Lance Goodman case isn't in my office. It's in the Feds hands."

"Anything I can do to cheer you up?"

The waiter returned with her glass of sake. She grabbed the shot glass and stared blankly for a few seconds then held it up to her mouth and downed the Japanese wine in one gulp.

"No thank you. I will be okay." She said.

We finished our sushi meals. Althea went into her small purse and pulled out a plastic means of payment and I told her to put it away. She insisted on paying for her meal at least. I asked her not to insult me and to put her plastic away. She looked at me intently with that *are you sure look*. I nodded and put two one hundred dollar bills inside the waiter's wallet.

After the waiter returned with my change, I left him a generous tip and we left the restaurant. The night air had changed and a cool breeze from the Pacific Ocean was in the air. As we started to walk Althea interlocked her left hand with my right hand and leaned against my shoulder. The sake I drank numbed my pain so it didn't hurt too much when she bumped up against me. This scene was much different than what I used to. She was sincerely holding my hand and not telling me lies I had paid to hear. I didn't want the night to end but I also knew not to push my luck out in public. I let out a fake yawn.

"Are you tired?" Althea asked.

"I didn't think I was."

"It's okay if you want to call it a night."

"I'm not ready to. I'll get a small coffee when we see a coffee shop."

"Do you like Starbucks?"

"No I prefer non brand name coffee shops."

"There are so many downtown. Patrick I have an idea."

"What is it?"

"I have a Keurig back at my place with a variety of coffee to choose from. What do you say?"

"Are you inviting me to your place?"

"Yes!"

"Are you sure?"

"Yes I trust you and when I ask you to leave I believe you'll be a gentleman."

"Of course I will be."

"Okay let's go. I parked in a garage on 4TH Street between Arizona Avenue and Santa Monica Boulevard."

I smiled and walked in the direction Althea led. As we walked up Arizona Avenue I saw two police cars without the sirens blaring coming our direction. I released Althea's hand and put my arm around her waist and rushed her along the sidewalk. I could tell she wasn't expecting that. We walked briskly towards the parking garage and I kept looking back after the cop cars passed us.

"Are you okay Patrick?"

"Yes!"

My paranoia was on high alert. We made it to the parking garage. Althea was parked on level 5. The lights of the same vehicle that brought us together lit up. She asked me if I wanted to drive. I declined and opened the driver's side door for her. I saw her reach across the middle console and open the passenger door for me. When we exited the parking garage Althea asked, "what radio station would you like to listen to?"

My mind was so blown at the fact that I was on a real date that her question didn't register. She repeated it. I told her I was fine with anything except country or heavy metal. She hit a button on her fancy steering wheel changing the radio until she stopped it on an old school R&B station. A young Stevie Wonder blasted through her car speakers singing about living just enough for the city and his father barely making a dollar. I immediately smiled at the tunes my ears heard. This music meant something. The message was so deep and not too far off from what was happening today.

Althea drove towards the 10 Freeway eastbound. The drive was quiet and the radio kept us company. It was that first date awkward moment. I wonder if she had changed her mind about me coming to her place. Would she politely ask me to call Uber when we get to her place? I was prepared. I was out of my league anyway.

We took the same exit off the 405 Freeway where Thad took his last breath. The exit broke our silence.

"The shooting took place not too far from here I was told." She said.

"Really? Any witnesses?" I asked cautiously.

"I'm not sure. Some innocent bystanders may have recorded something on their phones. I'll know more when I return to work."

"I'm sure they'll catch whoever did it." I said.

"We'll see. I apologize for bringing it up again on our date."

"No problem. I could tell at the restaurant it shook you up."

"Thanks Patrick!"

We turned into a gated parking garage a few blocks from the Howard Hughes Center. The building had 6 levels with condos and underground parking. Althea parked and before exiting she turned and looked at me with a smile on her face. Walking towards the elevators our fingers interlocked once more. As much I was enjoying the evening I was nervous as a high school kid on prom night.

Inside the elevator Althea pressed her key card against the panel and hit button number 6. I felt my phone vibrating. I pulled out my phone and I saw it was Townsend. I let the call go to voicemail. When we reached level 6 I followed Althea to a corner unit. She looked at me just before opening her door.

"I hope you're not crazy Patrick?"

"If you're having second thoughts I can call Uber."

"No I'm not. Please come in."

Her condo was well decorated with fine art on the walls. Her kitchen looked like a setting out of a home magazine. I saw a baby grand piano in the living room by a large window. I asked if she played. She told me she hadn't played in a while. I saw a small dining table with 4 chairs. It looked like her condo was a 2 bedroom but I didn't ask. She broke the silence and asked me to excuse her for a few minutes. I asked her, "where should I sit?"

"Make yourself at home. I'll be right back."

"Ok thanks."

I sat on the sofa and waited for her to return. There was a television hanging on the wall with a cable box and DVD player on a shelf beneath the television. I saw pictures of her and her brother from various trips they've taken. I saw an older couple in a picture frame I assume were her parents. They looked happy and in love. I saw her certificates of diplomacy on display amongst the pictures and a lot of books. Some I heard of and some I hadn't.

"Can I offer you something to drink?" she asked.

"Sure. What do you have?"

"I don't drink so whatever I have is left over from my family's last visit."

As she walked by to the kitchen I noticed she had changed into a pair of black yoga pants and her alumni t-shirt. I stood up and walked over to her kitchen counter.

"I have two beers, some Vodka and some scotch."

"I'll take a beer."

Her yoga pants and t-shirt revealed the curves and body definition her business attire kept hidden. It was evident Althea was athletic and took care of her body. When she handed me the beer she grabbed a bottle of water and protein bar. She remained standing and turned on the

TV.

"Anything you want to watch?" She asked.

My mind was still on her body. I wanted her and her body.

"Anything but a reality show." We both laughed.

"What's the last movie you saw?"

"It's been so long, I can't remember."

"Are you a comedy, action, murder or drama kind of person?"

"Any of those are cool."

"How about that one with Kevin Hart and the Rock?"

"Sure."

She sat down on the couch next to me but not too close and scrolled through the movies on demand until she found the movie.

"Do you need anything before the movie starts?"

"No I'm ok."

"Okay."

She stretched out and her feet touched my left leg. The sound of the TV kept the silence at bay as we sat there extending our date that should have ended in Santa Monica. I looked at Althea and she was relaxed looking at the TV. When the movie started Althea changed her position and sat up next to me.

"Do you mind?" she asked.

"No it's fine."

She rested her head on my shoulder and touched my hand.

"Patrick, You need a manicure."

"What makes you think I get manicures?"

"It's obvious you don't. That's why I said you need one."

"I keep my nails cut and I wash my hands."

"Seriously? Is that from a commercial? Would you get one if I paid for it?"

"I don't need your money."

We both laughed before getting back to the movie. She kept rubbing my hand then she touched my face. She didn't comment on my skin but I felt her looking at me. I looked away from the TV and Althea leaned in and kissed me. I wasn't prepared nor expecting that. She held the sides of my face in her soft hands and kissed me again. I remember seeing Kevin Hart standing in a gym with a high top fade before we disappeared to her bedroom. We kissed a little but didn't hug. We pulled at each other's clothes but not enough to take anything off.

"Patrick….I"

"I should just go." I said.

"I don't want you to."

"What should we do?" I asked.

It felt awkward.

"I don't know why I kissed you." She said.

"I didn't mind."

"You must think I'm easy." She said.

"I'm in no position to judge you. We're adults."

"Are you sure?"

"Yes."

She kissed the side of my face again and I felt her hand by the seat of my pants. I didn't need any more hints. She wanted to have sex. I lifted her t-shirt over her head and her breasts were sitting in C cups. I looked at her smooth skin. I touched her shoulders. Her skin was tight and ink free. I slid one of the straps down her shoulder and one of her breast became exposed. Her nipple was a caramel brown tone. I squeezed it tight and she flinched. I apologized. She told me it was okay. I had to remember I wasn't in my normal setting. Althea took my shirt off and rubbed my chest. I was glad the lights were off because if she had seen my wounds the sexual buzz would have been killed. We kissed a little more but that was the extent of the foreplay. She unzipped my pants and I felt her warm hands searching for my dick. She kissed me some more and started stroking my dick. I was still playing with her breasts. She felt my dick growing in her hand. We made eye contact.

"Patrick there's a ceramic box on my dresser that says *health and financial advisor.* Get a condom out of there please."

I turned around and looked on her dresser and like she said her advisor had four condoms inside. I grabbed one without thinking how many men had spoken to her advisor. When I turned back around Althea was lying on her bed with only her panties on. I took my jeans and boxers off and moved to the bed. The awkwardness was slowly killing the buzz. What I was used to wasn't happening in this bedroom. I don't know what Althea was used to. When I laid next to her she kissed me again and grabbed my dick once more. Oral sex wasn't an option clearly. I softly started rubbing her pussy from the outside of her panties. The whole scene was boring to me because I didn't know anything about affection. I just wanted to fuck and get it over with. My dick was now hard enough to roll the condom on so I sat up and opened the pack. She saw what I was doing and took her panties off. I climbed on top of her and she opened her legs slightly. When I slid my dick inside I felt her squirm a little but I didn't stop. I was going all the way in no turning back. Her body was so stiff and my strength was tested. I lifted one of her legs and started to stroke a little harder. I heard my first honest moan in years. Althea's eyes were closed as I worked her pussy as gentle as I could. I wanted to pull her hair and bite her nipples. I wanted to turn her over and slam right into her pussy and smack her ass. She didn't even touch me. She kept her hands up by her ears. I lifted her other leg onto my shoulders and pounded her a little harder. I could tell she wasn't used to this. Her moans told her story and the tightness of her pussy didn't lie. I wanted her to get on top so bad but I dare not interrupt the limited groove. We stayed in the missionary position until I came inside the condom. She opened her eyes as I let her legs down and moved to the side of her. We didn't hug or kiss anymore. The darkness in her room held us prisoner. We didn't speak.

I left Althea's around 3 AM. When my Uber driver turned into the small driveway of my motel in Hawthorne I had this discomforting feeling that all of my belongings had been stolen. I opened the door to see everything was still in place. I had to find another place to lay low. After thinking about it I realized my best choice would be to rent a Vacation Rental by Owner home. VRBO was a privately owned rental website that offered condos, villas, and homes for rent. The rental rates were comparable to hotels with the added benefit of "privacy". You paid by credit card and communicated through email over the internet. Some listings had pictures of the owners by their profile. No guarantee it was the actual owner. After you found a listing you liked, booked your dates and paid you received a confirmation email with check-in instructions. You didn't have any physical communication.

I drove to the local bookstore on Rosecrans Avenue to search the home rental website for a small place. The bookstore had Wi-Fi so I parked in the parking lot and use their free services. When I pulled into the parking lot I saw quite a few cars. The bookstore was closed but some of the other stores had nighttime workers restocking. I powered up one of the laptops. I found the free connection amongst several other protected connections in the area. The Internet browser opened up to MSN and at the top was a red banner headline talking about me still at large and dangerous. The Internet headline urged every citizen to remain on high alert for me. I typed in the website to begin my search. What city did I want to live in? Did I want a beach view? A pool? A condo? A house? How many bedrooms? How many bathrooms? I laughed to myself snapping out of my trance. I wasn't going on vacation. I needed a place to hide. I did need to select a city though. I sat there thinking of all the places in Los Angeles I'd most likely not be spotted, better yet identified. As I scrolled the listing my cell phone buzzed. I looked at the screen. It was Townsend. Now that I have my grown man pants on, he's concerned. I ignored his call and continued viewing the available listings. My cell phone buzzed again. It was from an unknown number. People who blocked their numbers annoyed me. I didn't answer. I found a listing in Hollywood Hills. The listing gave a map location but not an address. You received that information after you reserved and paid for the dates you selected. I pulled out the credit card connected to my alias and paid. It was three bedrooms, three and a half bathroom house. I saw Althea and I lying by the pool in the backyard behind the privacy gates and away from my criminal world. How long would I be able to live this lie? I wanted the chance to live my life over with her. I would put my past behind me and never look back. I would be Patrick. It would be easy. Wasn't that who Althea thought I was anyway? Then, that's who I would be. I exited the public library parking lot headed to my new home. I drove the whole way in silence. I thought about Catalina. Thinking of her meant I had to communicate with Townsend. I wasn't ready to do that yet.

The email I received from the listings owner gave me the address and the code to the lockbox. The street was wider than normal and only had a couple of cars parked on the street. The street lights didn't give off much light. I drove slowly looking at the house numbers. The house I was looking for had an odd number. Those houses were on the left side of the street. When I reached the address given, I saw a black tall wrought iron gate. I turned into the short driveway and left my car running. I got out of the car and saw the lockbox to the right of the gate. I punched in the code from the email and pulled the small lever open. Inside there was a set of keys and 2 remotes labeled garage and front gate. I closed the lockbox and press the remote for the front gate. The tall gate slowly opened inward and I drove my car inside. After I drove past the gate I waited for it to close behind me before I proceeded to the house. The gate was about 50 yards from the house. It was dark so I couldn't see the layout of the lot. I parked and unlocked the front door. My paranoia walked in with me as my hand grabbed the 9MM gun rested in the small of my back. I took a tour of the place. The furnishings looked new. The guest bedrooms looked comfortable. Not that I would be having sleepovers. The sheets on the bed were clean as were the towels in the Jack and Jill bathroom. The master bedroom had a king sized bed and a sitting area with a large screen television on the wall. There was a large glass door that opened to the backyard and a view of the pool. I walked to the kitchen. I opened the cabinets and saw glasses, plates, pots and pans. The refrigerator was empty. I wouldn't chance going to the grocery store. I made a mental note to order some groceries online. I had already decided that Althea would spend the night without thinking about what she might want. I couldn't accept the fact that she might not want the same thing as I did. It was a foreign thought in my mind, like an unwanted intruder and I dismissed it quickly. *I always get what I want. This time wouldn't be any different.*

I pulled out my cell phone to call Townsend. I had only one question for him. I knew he wouldn't answer it without first asking his own. My response to his question one down and one to go wouldn't be satisfactory so I knew he wasn't going to tell anything about Catalina. I didn't feel like dealing with it so I called Althea instead.

"Hi Patrick! How are you?" she asked.

"I'm well. How are you?"

"I'm ok."

"You sure?"

She didn't mention what happened the night before but I felt the awkwardness on the phone. An old girlfriend told me to always call the morning after you've had sex with a woman. This concept was foreign to me because the women I 'd slept with didn't have emotional needs. They had non-negotiable hourly rates. Simple as that!

"Patrick...."

More silence. I broke the silence.

"It's ok. We're both adults and I respect you. I know you're a lady and not one of those other things." I laughed.

"It's not funny Patrick."

"Actually it is."

"Why is it funny?"

"I've never seen a small jar like that on a woman's dresser." I laughed again.

"Well I think it's classy to have that instead of reaching inside a nightstand drawer rummaging through papers and God knows what else."

We laughed a few minutes more before I asked her if I could see her again this evening. She was hesitant, still ashamed perhaps. I enjoyed her company and wanted more of it. Not necessarily sex but genuine female company. The silence seemed like an eternity. "Ok but under one condition." She said.

"What's that?"

"I get to see where you live and we're not having sex."

"Deal! What time should I pick you up?"

"Do you mean send Uber?" she laughed.

"Ha ha!"

"I'll drive my own car just in case you get frisky."

"I was a gentleman last night."

"Yes you were. Maybe I don't trust myself. What's your address Patrick?"

I didn't remember the address. I had to quickly pull up the email to give it to her.

"And another thing?" she said.

"You said one condition. You're already at 2!" I laughed.

"Anyway! I want you to cook for me."

"No problem. What cuisine do you have in mind?"

"Something Italian."

"Italian it is. See you around 7 PM?"

"That works for me."

Damn! I had scheduled another *date*. I powered up my laptop and found a grocery delivery site. I ordered enough food to make it look like I actually lived there. I saw the instruction for the television, satellite dish, the surround sound and the lights for the pool. The home alarm system instructions were there as well. I hid the sheet of paper inside my laptop bag. It was second nature for a woman to snoop around a man's place.

I spent the morning getting acquainted with my new hideaway and waiting for my grocery delivery. I did a light workout. I turned the TV on for the first time since I'd moved in. I'd been avoiding it because I didn't want to see my face plastered all over the news. One of those dumb talk shows I hated so much was about to go off the air with early afternoon news to follow. I sat down on the sofa and waited, certain of what was about to follow. The newscasters appeared on the screen.

"Here's Amanda Tgyuen with the latest on the murders near the 405 freeway in LA."

"Thank you, David. I'm here with Detective John Valentine. Detective, what's the latest on the hunt for the killer or killers of Thaddeus?"

"No killers, only one killer, Lance Goodman. His fingerprints were found on the passenger side door and on the inside of the door hinge."

"You're certain he had no accomplices?"

"The public needs to know Lance Goodman is a very dangerous man. We have no doubt that he's somewhere in

the L.A. vicinity. Extreme caution is warranted."

My picture suddenly appeared on the screen.

"If you see this man, please call 555-767-2366. This is Amanda Tgyuen reporting."

My face was plastered all over the television screen for everyone to see. Had Althea seen it already? Was she this very minute trying to decide whether or not to turn me in to the cops? I had known this was coming, but I had avoided thinking about it. I refused to hide, though.

I wondered what Althea would think. How would she feel knowing when she received the call about Thad's death she was having dinner with the killer? Would she still be talking to me? No! I had to be someone else for her. I had to be a man she would be proud to be with. I had to be Patrick, but I had no idea who he really was. I knew Lance! He was a man who killed for money, nothing about that spelled love. I didn't want to call Townsend but I needed him. I needed a new car.

"Your face is plastered all over the news." He said.

"I know!"

"What have you been doing for the last twelve hours?"

"I've been busy."

"Three people identified you as the man they saw fire

into a dark sedan yesterday evening. Where are you?"

"Hollywood Hills."

"I told you that you didn't have a lot of time."

"I know. I need a car."

"I'm not coming to Hollywood Hills!"

"Where can you meet me?"

"I think you should stay put."

"I can't. I have a date with someone."

"A date? Are you serious right now Lance?"

"Can you meet me with a car or not?"

The silence between us was choking me. I knew he'd never understand. For years I've never seen Townsend display any emotions.

"Meet me in Inglewood at the casino in two hours." He shouted and hung up.

I headed into the bedroom, got dressed, grabbed my phone and went out to my car. I had 5 hours or so before meeting up with Althea. I entered the freeway to meet Townsend. My plan was to get the new car with minimal conversation. On the way I thought about Althea and Catalina. I had to find Catalina. I figured Maison knew, but he was keeping his mouth shut. I needed Sydney to really get into her new acting role. I thought she was hesitating and that was something I wouldn't tolerate. I wanted her to get closer to Maison Chambers so I could get what I wanted; him. Sydney owed me. The next thing I knew I was texting her. "Meet me at Hank's bar in an hour."

She was twenty minutes late and looked like she wanted to be anywhere but with me. I wondered what was going on. Was she trying to get out of doing what I paid her to do? Maybe I should remind her who I was and what I was capable of.

"Why did you want to see me?" she asked. "I have plans for later."

"Cancel them." I said

"I saw your face plastered all over the news again today. Do you think it's okay for you to be seen in public?"

"Let me worry about that. What have you been doing?"

"I've been busy trying to figure out how to get to this guy Maison."

"And? How's that coming?"

"It's coming along."

"You're moving too slow. You need to step it up!"

"Don't talk to me that way."

"The sooner you finish, the sooner you get the rest of your money."

"I know that."

"It's time you and Maison Chambers got to know each other better."

"You need to explain what you mean?"

I felt sick just thinking about Maison Chambers. I wanted him dead and it didn't make any difference to me how that happened. I wanted him to suffer in pain until his last breath. If that meant Sydney disrespecting herself in the process, I didn't care.

"What if I've changed my mind?"

"Do you still have the money I gave you?"

"I used to think it would be easy, but I'm not so sure anymore."

"Do you have my money?"

"Is that all you're concern about? Your money?"

"If you're reconsidering that's the only thing I'm concerned about. Come on, you can do it."

I needed her so bad for this one thing.

"Listen, I have plans for later tonight. I have to go."

I glared at her. "You aren't going anywhere." Hank's bar was one of the most popular dive bars in downtown LA. The wall to wall people at the bar was proof of that. I wondered if coming here had been a good idea. When I saw a thin guy wearing a dark blue jacket staring at me I wondered if he had recognized me. Had he seen my face plastered on the cover of a newspaper or on the news? Of course he could have. No doubt I was a suspect on the run and the cops were looking for me. Why was the guy at the bar staring at me? For the last few minutes he hadn't taken his eyes off me. Could he be a cop and was he trying to decide if I was who he thought I was? I turned in my chair so that now all he had was a view of my side profile. Sydney was nursing her drink and her eyes were on my face with a curious expression on hers. It almost looked like she wanted to ask me a question, but the question hadn't quite formed in her mind. Then, she noticed I was looking in the direction of the bar and her eyes followed mine. I thought she looked a little frightened and that was the last thing I wanted. In a situation like this the last thing I needed was for her to show any fear.

"Do you think he recognizes you?" she asked. "I don't know, but I'm not going to take any chances. We're leaving. When I get up, you get up like nothing's wrong. Don't draw any attention to yourself."

"He recognizes you. I'm scared."

"Shut up and do what I just told you to do."

We headed for the door and did not look back. When we were safely outside, I saw the guy hadn't budged and wasn't looking at me. He was talking to the woman standing next to him. Why was I becoming paranoid? I had outsmarted everyone for a long time and would continue to. I had to focus on Sydney so I could get Maison. She was leisurely redoing her lipstick, always worried about how she looked. It made sense, she was an actress and her looks were her ticket to stardom. She was hungry for it and I knew she would do anything. This thing with Maison would prove that she had the acting chops she needed. I grabbed her hand and we began to walk down S. Grand Avenue. I kept up my tirade about Maison.

"Was there a problem when you talked to him the last time? Is that what the problem is?" "He's creepy." Sydney said and laughed.

"What's so funny?" I asked.

"You are. Don't worry I'll give him a call. Maybe I'll even go to his office."

"This is serious! I don't care, just do it."

"Killing Thad seems to have rattled your nerves." Sydney said.

"I feel great. Now it's time to get into your new acting role. You're a successful real estate investor and you deal in high-end properties for architectural firms. Start thinking about it like your life depends on it."

Sudden fear shadowed her brown eyes. "Are you

threatening me?"

"Of course not, but I don't want you to have any doubts about what you're supposed to do."

Ten minutes later Sydney and I went our separate ways. I was on my way to see Townsend and she told me she was going to call Maison and set up another meeting. She was young and inexperienced and he was totally ruthless. Of course, she had offered herself up for this and I should remember that. He would kill her instantly if he suspected anything, but I had to trust that she wouldn't take any unnecessary chances. Then, the devil made his presence known again reminding me that it needed to be done. Sometimes we had no choice. "Take care of yourself. Maison has to die." That was the evil voice in my head. All I knew was that I had to get Maison and Sydney was going to help me. Even though things seem to be going exceptionally well with Althea, I couldn't truly move on until I killed Maison. I got back on the freeway towards Inglewood to meet Townsend. I began to wonder if I would ever be free? Would I spend the rest of my life running, one step ahead of whoever was trying to find me? I had begun to hope for a real life, a life that might or might not include Althea, but I had some doubts. What woman would want a life with me? I had no idea.

Sydney.

She dialed Maison Chamber's number. A woman answered on the first ring, almost as if she'd been expecting her call.

"Maison Chambers." Sydney asked.

The woman had a deep Southern accent. "Is Mr. Chambers expecting your call?"

"Yes, he is."

"One moment, please. Whom may I say is calling."

"Tell him it's Sydney."

"Maison!"

"Thank you for taking my call, Maison."

"Any time. So, what can I do for you Sydney?"

"We need to continue our discussion."

"Alright, come to my office tomorrow morning at eleven. I should have time for you then."

"Right, ok." Sydney said.

She felt so insecure at that moment she wondered how she would get through the meeting. How could she have gotten involved with people like Lance and now Maison? Lance had her cornered. She had to do what he wanted. He had paid her a lot of money and she needed the money to pay her rent, other living expenses and for more acting lessons. She was hungry to make it as an actress, to prove to herself she could be successful in film. She had to think of what she was doing for Lance as her first serious acting role. She would get into character by dressing in the only suit she owned to look like the businesswoman she wanted to convince Maison she was. She went to her closet and chose a grey suit and paired it with a light blue blouse. The skirt reached just above her knees and was the most ladylike outfit she owned. She slipped on a conservative pair of black pumps with a two-inch heel. She looked in a full-length mirror in her one bedroom apartment and thought she looked exactly the way she wanted to look, like a businesswoman. The problem was she didn't feel like herself. She felt awkward and unnatural. Then, she remembered she was playing a character. Besides if she had gone to the meeting wearing a skirt up to her ass Maison might become interested in her in a way she didn't want. Sydney suspected Lance had other ideas in his head about how she could convince Maison she was a real investor, but she didn't want to play his game. Then she thought about the money and realized her morals were for sale. In a real sense the $50,000 he was going to pay her was the one thing in her life that kept her getting up each morning.

Precisely at 11:00 a.m. the next morning she found herself riding the elevator to Maison Chamber's office.

Lance had called late last night and had her go over everything she planned to say to Maison. He wanted everything to go right and he wanted to know everything she planned to say. They ran lines as if they were rehearsing for a show. When she got to the seventh floor, the elevator door opened onto the reception area. She introduced herself and the receptionist a pretty blonde who looked up at her. "Mr. Chambers will see you now."

Sydney thanked the young receptionist and opened the double glass doors. She had to make sure her nervousness wasn't obvious to Maison. When she walked into his office he was sitting at his desk with a stack of papers in front of him and he didn't even look up at her. She felt as though she may as well have been a piece of furniture in his office. He was on a call, but the person on the other end did most of the talking. She fiddled with her purse and kept clasping and unclasping her hands. Finally, she took a couple of deep breaths knowing she had to stay calm or he might see right through her. Finally he put his cell phone down on his desk.

"Good to see you Sydney. Are you here to talk about that property again?"

"Yes, well I don't understand why you aren't taking me seriously. At least you could take me to see it so I can make an offer. Are you free now?"

"I might be."

"What does that mean? Either you are or you aren't."

"Let's have lunch." Maison said.

"It's not even eleven-thirty." Sydney said.

"We'll have a drink first, then."

They walked a few blocks to Maison's favorite restaurant on Palmetto Street and went inside. The place had just opened and they were the first patrons to arrive that day and there was no hostess to show them to a table. Instead Maison took Sydney's arm and led her to the bar.

"The bartender isn't here." Sydney said."

"I'll make the drinks." Maison said and began to walk behind the bar.

"No, you won't." Sydney said.

"Right." he said when he saw the bartender walking towards them."

"The usual, Mr. Chambers?" the bartender asked.

"Vodka on the rocks and the lady will have a glass of wine," he turned to Sydney. "Red or white?"

"Red is fine."

They took their drinks to a table and sat there for a few moments with Sydney trying not to look at Maison while he didn't remove his eyes from her face. It made her even more uncomfortable than she already was, but she had to assume the role of an experience businesswoman and overcome her nerves.

"How can you drink straight vodka?" she asked. "It tastes awful."

"Let's just say it's an acquired taste and not everyone can cultivate it."

To Sydney, he sounded like a snob. If he even suspected her connection to Lance, he'd probably have her killed. It was just another fact she kept playing over in her head, a thought she shouldn't be thinking. Maison was still staring at her and when she looked at him Sydney thought there was nothing behind his eyes. His soul was empty and she realized that when she looked at Lance she saw the same expression.

"When will you take me to see the property?" she asked.

He kept staring at her for a few moments as if deciding what he could gain by showing the property to her. Sydney was certain he never did anything unless it would benefit him in some way and she was wondering what he thought he would gain by taking her to see the property. She wasn't sure, but it made her uncomfortable.

"How about Thursday night around 6 PM?" he asked.

"I can do that." she said.

"Good. Now what do you want for lunch?"

When I got close to the casino I called Townsend to see if he was there and where he was parked. He answered on the second ring with attitude.

"I'm on the back row closest to Prairie Avenue in a black Charger." He said.

I hung up and kept making my way up Century Boulevard. The parking lot was at its normal capacity – full. I drove through the lot at a slow speed looking for the first opening to turn and head to the back row. When I reached the back row I made a right towards the Forum. About 30 yards down I saw one car with its taillights on. That was Townsend. When I pulled up Townsend got out.

"Do you have everything out of the car?" he asked.

"Yep!"

He sized me up. "Cool!" Then he handed me the keys to my new set of wheels and extended his hand for the keys I had. Our eyes deadlocked on each other and silent. I tossed the keys to him and he walked to the driver's side got in and drove off. Our relationship was at odds because of my mental state. It is what it is. I got into my new car and headed towards the freeway back to Hollywood Hills.

It troubled me that Townsend and I were not on the best of terms. After all he had dropped everything to come to my aid. I was appreciative but I didn't plan on meeting Althea. I hadn't planned on developing feelings for her. I didn't think it would take this long to kill Maison. My head felt like a category 4 hurricane was going through it. It was time to put an end to my misery; kill Maison. Sydney needed to increase her interest for the property to gain his interest. I called Sydney.

"How did it go?" I asked.

"Fine, he's taking me to see the property later this week."

"I'm assuming you have your story ready to go."

"Not exactly. Let's just say it's in development."

"Make sure you have everything straight in your mind. There can't be any slip ups. If there are Maison will catch them and that wouldn't be good for you."

"I don't like the sound of that."

"Just do what I tell you to do and you'll be fine."

Sydney decided that she was going to make things work with Maison that day. They were meeting at his office at 6:00 p.m. and from there he would take her to the property was located at 925 Wilshire Blvd and the little research she had done told her that it was perfect for the story she had concocted for Maison, that her client owned a large architectural firm, was expanding his business and looking for a larger workspace. She had no idea where the idea of an architectural firm came from. Maison was a business contact who had a property one of her best and most well-paying clients was interested in. That was it. She concentrated on that and nothing else. She meditated for a few minutes and that helped her let go of any fear she had regarding the situation. Maison was no longer a threat to her. He was merely a means to an end for her. What she wanted more than anything was the money and he was going to help get it for her. Again, she dressed conservatively, a black suit she had bought the day before and a nice white blouse.

She looked at herself in the mirror and thought she looked just right for the role she was going to play. With the outfit, she wore a plain gold necklace with matching bracelet. Her makeup was subdued and as she took once last glanced at herself she knew she would be able to pull of the role of a successful real estate investor because she looked the part. Sydney arrived at Maison's office twenty minutes later and she was early. Soon, she found herself standing behind the same glass doors and facing his young receptionist.

"I'll tell Mr. Chambers you're here." the receptionist said.

Sydney took a seat on the brown leather sofa. "Thank you."

She sat down and waited, but after about ten minutes she began to grow impatient. Was Maison keeping her waiting on purpose? Was he hoping to fray her nerves so she would lose her confidence? That would never happen. He had no idea how determined she was to see this through to the end successfully. She wanted two things; the money and to prove to herself that she was a good actress. When she auditioned for roles in the future she would remember this day. Finally, Maison came out of his office and greeted her with a big smile and a hug, *you phony bastard, Sydney thought.*

"Are we set to go?" Maison asked.

"You lead the way." Sydney said.

She took his arm and they headed outside where his driver was waiting to take them to the property. No words were exchanged between the two of them and Sydney wondered if she should say something, but didn't. She had always felt uneasy with him probably because every few minutes she'd catch him leering at her. Maybe he thought his attitude wasn't obvious, but it absolutely was. They pulled up in front of the building and Maison's driver, got out, opened the door and they stepped out onto the sidewalk.

"Come back for us in an hour." Maison said to the driver.

They walked towards the front door of the building and ever the gentleman he held the door for her. *What a phony you are, Sydney thought.* She gave him her prettiest smile and they entered the lobby of the three story building.

"You haven't told me much about your client," Maison said. "What does he need this building for?"

"He has an architectural firm, has three offices, one in Houston, one in San Francisco and one in Los Angeles, but business is growing and he needs a larger space. He's also thinking of opening an office in Long Island, New York."

"We have property available there."

"He's anxious to close this deal because he wants to make the move as soon as possible. I've told him what you want for the building and he has agreed to pay the asking price."

Maison snapped his fingers. "Just like that, we have a deal."

Suddenly, Sydney felt uneasy. She expected Maison to ask more questions about her client, but he agreed to everything. She couldn't believe he'd done that without an ulterior motive. What did he want? She knew it had to be something and she felt certain she would find out soon enough.

"I'll need to meet with your client before any papers are signed." Maison said.

"Of course, I'll make the arrangement." Sydney said.

"Have him come to my office. My attorney will draw up the necessary papers."

He pulled her close for a quick hug and she was suddenly very uncomfortable. There was something about him that made her more than a little uncomfortable. She hoped he understood this was about business and nothing else. The next words out of his mouth and she realized he was interested in more.

"How about having dinner with me on Friday night to celebrate this deal?" he asked.

"I'll have to check my schedule," she said.

"Don't you eat dinner? I'll take you to Cut, a new restaurant in L.A. The beef dishes are delicious. I'll pick you up at eight on Friday night."

She couldn't wait to get away from him because she suddenly felt slimy as if she'd rolled around in some garbage. She would discuss this with Lance and see what he had to say. No doubt he'd want her to go on the date, but then he wouldn't have to sit across from a degenerate and try to pretend he was having a good time.

"Call me, Maison, okay? I'm probably free, but I'm not certain."

He leaned in for a kiss, but she turned her head and his lips landed on her chin. "Til Friday." He said.

She was relieved to see him disappear inside the building and walked the block to where her car was parked. As soon as she sat down, she called Lance and he answered immediately and she knew he had been waiting for her call.

"How did it go?" I asked.

"I have to set up a meeting between him and my client."

"Wait a minute." She said. She looked in her rear view mirror and saw a man she was certain was Maison walking down the street. If it was him and he saw her he might get suspicious.

"I have to go," she said to Lance.

She pulled out of the parking spot and drove for a few minutes and called Lance again. She heard the anger in his voice when he answered the phone.

"What was that all about?"

"I thought Maison was following me and I didn't want

him to find me talking on the phone. He makes me feel creepy anyway, like I need to take a bath every time I see him."

"What's the matter Sydney? You don't like my good friend Maison?" I laughed loudly.

"Stop laughing Lance. I did what you wanted me to do, but I never want to see him again. You're going to have to figure out what to do next, like coming up with someone to pass off as my client."

"I'm sorry Sydney; you're not finished with him yet. You won't be until I say you are."

"Where are you going to find someone to act as my client?"

"Don't worry about that."

"No one could ever get anything passed you, Lance," she said. "Now, Maison asked me to have dinner with him on Friday night and I refuse to go."

"You have to go!" Lance said.

"I can't sit across from him for an entire meal without screaming. I refuse to socialize with him. He's creepy and makes my skin crawl."

"This will all be over soon and you'll never have to see him or me again. It's only a couple of hours of your life. Do you know where he's taking you?"

"He's making reservations at Cut."

"Tell him you'll go."

"I think he's got something else in mind."

"You're a big girl. You can handle him."

At the time Sydney thought Maison was following her he was actually on the phone with his attorney talking to him about checking to see if she was a legitimate investor. His instincts had told him that she might be someone other than who she claimed to be. Sure she had shown him a business card that looked legit, but she could have gotten them anywhere. She dressed the part too, but underneath her business suits he saw a whore.

Of course, the only woman he didn't view as a slut was his mother. While he waited for his attorney to pick up the phone, he thought about Lance, certain he was responsible for four murders that had taken place a couple of days ago. All he knew was that the victims were all male, and one was a L.A. cop. The way the crime had been described sounded like Lance's handiwork. Maison gave his attorney Sydney's name and told him to do a background check on her.

"I want to know everything." He said.

His lawyer called back a couple of hours later. "She's legit." He said. "She's associated with one of the top real estate companies in LA. She's been with them seven years and is one of their top agents with a great history of A list clientele."

Maison laughed.

"I would make the deal. You've been sitting on this property for a while now." His attorney said.

"Thanks for the information."

On the same night Maison and Sydney had dinner plans, I had plans with Althea and although I knew I should have canceled them I didn't. At 7:00 p.m. on the dot the intercom system in my Hollywood Hills hideaway rang.

"Yes!" I said.

"It's Althea, Patrick."

I knew it was her from the security camera. She looked so sexy standing there with a light brown sundress on with a wedge sandal. Her pearly whites showing for the camera but she didn't know it.

"Hi! I will buzz you in. Drive up to the house and I'll open the garage for you to park inside."

"Okay. Thanks."

I walked through the kitchen to the entry of the garage and pressed the button to open the garage door for Althea. She hurried out of her car.

"Oh you fancy!" she said.

"Not at all. Welcome." I said.

She approached the entry. "Do I need to take my shoes off?" she asked with a smile.

"No you don't have to. Get in here."

She stared into the kitchen. "Is this your house? Are we having dinner here?"

"Yes, I hope that's alright with you."

"Am I being punked? She looked around to see if someone was going to jump out."

"You're funny. No you're not being punked."

She looked around, took a few steps into the living room, impressed by the furniture and the way the living space looked. "Very nice. You have good taste, Patrick."

"May I offer you something to drink? I have white and red wine. I have some rum from Central America, coke and water."

"I'll take a glass of red wine please."

"Sure."

I had no idea where the wine bottle opener was. Lucky for me when I opened the drawer near the stove there was an opener inside the drawer with other utensils. I poured Althea's glass of wine and told her I needed to get dinner started. She made a smirk like *yeah right.*

"So Patrick what restaurant did you order take out

from?"

"You're funny. Feel free to check the kitchen as I start to cook. There's no take out here."

"Oh yeah?" she started walking around the kitchen counter.

I didn't stop her. I reached in the cabinet under the countertop and pulled out a couple of pans and a skillet. I pulled out some spices from the top cabinet. She was standing there watching in disbelief. I didn't say anything I just kept preparing something Italian like she asked for.

"So where did you learn how to cook Patrick? Can you cook?"

"Someone near and dear to my heart!" I smiled.

"Your mother?"

My facial expression changed. It displayed a frown now.

"No!"

"Your grandmother?"

"I didn't have the pleasure of spending much time with her."

I turned the back burner on to boil some water for the penne pasta. I could see the wheels turning in that educated head of hers. I continued cutting the little bit of fat from the chicken breast.

"Now I'm worried. Maybe you can't cook." She laughed.

"Oh trust me I can cook."

"That remains to be seen. Or should I say *tasted*."

"You'll enjoy it. I'm sure of it."

"Ok Mr. Patrick."

I don't know what made me do it but I moved in to kiss her. Maybe it was the way she said Mr. Patrick or the way her lips moved after she took a sip of her wine. When I got close Althea didn't move away and my lips touched hers so passionately that I almost knocked the cutting board with the chicken onto the floor.

I hadn't kissed a female in so long I had forgotten the realness of its effect. She closed her eyes but I kept mine opened. I looked at her as our lips stayed pressed together and thought I could really start over. I could say the hell with Maison. Pay Sydney the remaining $25,000. Ask Townsend one last time about Catalina. Move Althea and I to another location (non-extradition) of course. There was only one problem. How would I tell Althea who I really was? Would I ever tell her? My fairytale dream ended as I felt her lips move away from mine.

"Patrick you're supposed to be cooking, remember?"

"Yes of course."

I continue prepping the dish I was going to make. I saw her wipe the lipstick under her lips and smile at me. I smiled back and turned on one of the front burners to cook the chicken. I added some spices to the chicken and set the burner on low. In another skillet I sautéed red and green peppers with onions. Then I poured some heavy cream and half and half into the skillet and mixed everything together. I turned the chicken breast. The water was boiling now so I added the penne pasta.

"Do you have any magazines?" she asked.

Shit I forgot to get house fillers like that.

"I'm sorry I don't do subscriptions."

"Not even a Sports Illustrated?"

Why was she pushing the magazine issue? I found myself getting annoyed and stirring the veggies so hard that some of them landed on the floor. I didn't bend down to pick them up. I wanted to finish this meal and get her the hell out of here as soon as possible.

"No I'm sorry." I replied.

"It's okay Patrick. I just didn't want you to feel uncomfortable with someone starring at you." Then she moved over to the couch and asked if she could turn on the TV. I felt the size of ant from my childish annoyance.

"Sure. The remote should be on the coffee table."

"Thanks."

I mixed the chicken breast in with the other veggies and checked on the boiling penne. The pasta was ready so I removed it from the burned and drained the water. After the Alfredo sauce thickened a bit I mixed everything together in one of the ceramic bowls.

"Althea would you like a salad?"

"Yes that would be great. What kind of dressing do you have?"

"Raspberry Balsamic Vinaigrette."

"Perfect."

Althea turned the TV to a financial channel that had a running stock ticker on the bottom of the screen and two people anchoring the show. I couldn't hear what they were saying. Looking at the channel made me think of Maison's account and how much had been transferred to the account I set up.

I made two salads with arugula lettuce, cherry tomatoes, craisins and a sprinkle of crushed walnuts. I didn't pour any dressing on the salads. I grabbed two plates from the cabinet and put a small portion of the chicken Alfredo penne pasta on both of our plates. I sat the plates and salads in place with the salad dressing and salt and pepper on the table.

"Dinner is served."

"It smells good Patrick. May I have some more wine please?"

"Yes. Can I get you anything else before I sit down?"

"No thanks. Let's taste your culinary skill Mr. Patrick."

She lowered head as she did before and crossed her heart when she finished her prayer. I didn't pray. I thought about Sydney's dinner meeting with Maison. I was beginning to worry that Sydney wouldn't be able to keep up the façade much longer. But I was here with Althea enjoying every minute of her presence. I could get use to this. I would have to pick up a few tabloids but other than that all is well with this. Althea took a few bites of her salad and then the pasta. I watched her lips as she chewed silently. She closed her eyes each time she took a bite of food. She looked so enchanting sitting here. I had barely touched my food when she broke me from my trance.

"Not bad Patrick. I must say I wasn't expecting you to cook. This is really good though."

"Thank you."

"I'll do the dishes Patrick."

"No you won't."

"It's the least I can do since you cooked."

"You're a guest. Relax."

I too was a guest in this rental home. After we finished eating, we went into the living room. I was becoming more comfortable with her every time we were together. She was smart and easy to talk to and much different than the whores I usually associated with. I had always thought it was a mistake to develop a real relationship with a woman since I felt certain if she learned the truth about me I would never see her again. I was also always worried about being turned into the police. Why did I think things would be different with Althea? I didn't really believe they would be, but I was beginning to feel something for her that I had never felt for any other woman since Londen. It didn't make me entirely comfortable, but there was nothing I could do about it and could only wait and see what happened.

"I'm going to San Francisco to visit my parents next weekend." she said.

"That sounds nice. How long has it been since you've seen them?" I asked.

"Three or four months. It's my father's birthday; he'll be sixty years old. Do you ever see your parents?"

"No." I responded curtly.

She looked at me, puzzled, but didn't speak and the

conversation about parents ended there. I was glad because I felt the devil inside me stirring. He was a restless fellow and the last thing I wanted was for him to make an appearance with Althea there. We sat there in silence for a little while and I found the silence more than a little uncomfortable. I thought that she was annoyed with me for some reason. I thought she wanted me to reveal things I just couldn't, at least not yet and maybe never. I wanted to be honest with her, but this was about as honest as I could be with her right now.

"I guess this is just the way you are." She suddenly said.

I looked straight at her. "I don't understand."

"You're very secretive. I mean I know so little about you and every time I ask you something I get the silent treatment."

"Are you talking about the fact that I won't discuss my parents with you? There are things I find difficult to talk about."

"It seems to me that includes everything. I don't understand. I still don't know who you are Patrick and I want to. Why don't you ever want to talk about yourself?"

"I'm a pretty boring guy."

"I doubt that."

"What do you want to know?"

"You told me you were a businessman. What kind of businesses are you involved in?"

"I own a couple of laundromats in Seattle and I'm also a partner in a start-up there too. I travel there a few times a month to see how things are going."

Her eyes seemed to light up. "So, you're like a silent partner."

"That describes my role very well."

"Why didn't you tell me that before?"

"When I'm with you I don't think much about business."

She smiled and touched my hand. I don't remember how we got into the bedroom, all I know is we were lying in each other's arms. I pressed my lips to hers; they were soft and hot at the same time. I slid my tongue into her mouth and she met it with her own. I wanted to possess her, but I had to go easy. After all, she was a lady, not some whore. Whores were all I knew and she was not a whore.

"Fuck me Patrick!" she said. Not what I expected. I unzipped her dress and it slipped down her body like it was several sizes too large. She slid down, and her hands grabbed my dick. Her nipples were as hard as diamond. I took one of her nipples into my mouth and cradled her other breast in my calloused palm. I rolled on a condom and began to ride her. I thrusted once cautiously, then again not too cautiously, and she began to move with me. I was lost in the heat and the curves of her body. She shouted, screamed and cried out my name. I reveled in her. I flipped her over onto her stomach and slid my hard dick in from behind. She glanced back at me with a look of sensual approval. I gasped at the wonder of it all. I was hard and mesmerized by her body and how she moved in sync with my stroke. It felt good knowing I hadn't paid for this. She was really into it. That was what I needed, to lose myself in her and feel something *real*.

She moved forward and lay me down on my back. Althea climbed on top of me and kissed my lips then ran her tongue down my body stopping at my hard dick which she took into her mouth. Her warm mouth felt incredibly good around my dick. She licked up and down the shaft of my dick so sensually I wanted to pay her. She massaged my hard dick a few minutes more before she slid my hardness inside her wet pussy. I sat up quickly noticing no condom had been put on. She pressed her fingers against my lips and pushed me back down on the bed.

I couldn't relax but her ride was slow and felt amazing. She raised and lowered her hips down on my hardness. Her eyes were closed and her hands on my chest as she continued her erotic ride. My dick felt the warmth of her pussy. It was deep, warm, and very wet. I moved my hips to meet her as she came down on my dick. We enjoyed our sexual encounter for an hour longer before Althea released and I felt her body shake frantically. She bit her bottom lip before kissing me again.

"Did you cum Patrick?"

"No I didn't."

"You didn't?" she asked with a puzzled look.

"I was close but you beat me."

"Do you want to go again?"

I definitely wanted to reach the sexual mountaintop but I was a little disturbed with the raw sex session that just took place. She seemed to be fine with it. I wasn't. That awkward moment was back with us. The silence and the darkness in the room made it worse. She eased off of me and laid on my shoulder rubbing my chest. I wasn't use to lying around. Normally my time was up and the employee with the online profile would get dressed and leave. I found myself actually holding her tightly. We still didn't say anything to each other. I felt her head get heavy. She was falling asleep. I heard her breathing a little heavier than normal. I looked down and her eyes were closed.

I slid from next to her and grabbed my cell phone. Sydney had texted me several times. From reading her text I felt she was starting to panic.

"Are you still with Maison."

She responded immediately.

"Yes. This creep wants to go for drinks. Lance I can't keep this up."

"Calm down Sydney. Where are you now?"

"We're at the restaurant. I'm in the ladies' room."

"Well get back to the table. Text me where you guys go for drinks."

"I didn't say I was going for drinks."

"Text me the place where you go next."

"I don't know Lance."

I didn't reply to her last text. I looked at Althea sleeping comfortably. I had a decision to make. Leave right now and head to L.A. to grab Maison or risk Sydney falling apart and getting killed. What would I tell Althea when she woke up and realized I wasn't there? I stood there tapping my right leg. I gathered up my clothes as quietly as I could. I saw Althea move a little but she didn't wake up.

I got dressed in the living room. I thought about leaving a note for her. I couldn't exactly say I was going out for some bread and milk. I grabbed my keys and walked through the kitchen to the garage. Damn she would hear the garage open. I stood in the doorway between the mud room and the garage. My mind danced back and forth from Sydney to Althea then back to Sydney then to Maison then back to Althea. I wanted Maison badly. I wanted Althea in my life just as bad. Maison took the lead in my thoughts and I hit the button to open the garage and ran to get into the Charger. I backed out quickly. I didn't see any lights come on quickly inside the house. When I reached the tall gate, I looked in the rearview mirror and the house still looked dark.

I stayed in front of the gate until it closed. I pulled out my cell phone and started to call Townsend but then decided against it. I texted Sydney instead.

"Where are you guys going next?"

"I don't know. I feel so uncomfortable right now."

"Keep it together just a little while longer. I'm on my way."

My cell phone started buzzing. It was Althea. What was I going to say? I had a few more rings before it went to voicemail. That wouldn't be good. My cell phone buzzed again.

"Hi sleeping beauty."

"Patrick where did you go? Why did you leave me in

this house alone?"

"I apologize. An emergency came up with a friend that needs my help."

"What kind of emergency?"

"They said it was life or death."

"You should have woken me up. I would've left when you left. I'm going home!"

"You looked so peaceful sleeping. Please don't leave. I won't be too long."

"Take all the time you need. I'm leaving."

I heard her moving around obviously getting dressed. "Althea please don't leave." I can't believe I was pleading with a woman to stay. The thought immediately took me back to Maxine begging the worthless human registered as my father not to leave. She didn't say anything. I was starting to feel a new beginning was 1 kill away for me. Who was I kidding? There was no guarantee Althea would be that new beginning.

"Althea?"

"What Patrick?"

"I'll call my friend and tell him I can't make it."

"Don't do that Patrick. Then I'd feel terrible if something happened to them."

My conscious would be fine. That was the risk I was

used to dealing with.

"I'm turning around Althea."

"No Patrick!"

I didn't say anything.

"Do you have anything besides man soap in your bathroom?"

I smiled. "I bought a 2 pack of Dove at the store."

"Oh really? You didn't know I was going to shower at your place."

"I was hoping you would."

"I hope everything is okay with your friend. Goodbye Patrick. I still may go home."

She wasn't completely committed to staying. I was annoyed.

"Ok Althea!" I said before hanging up.

Sydney had sent me two more text saying they were heading to the SoHo House. That was perfect I could be there in twenty minutes or less at this hour. I took the Sunset Boulevard exit and slowed down my speeds and gathered my composure. The moment I had been waiting for was minutes away. The upscale lounge required a membership and I wasn't dressed to impress so I would need Sydney a little longer than I knew she was ready for. I parked on the opposite side of the street and watched the

LA LA Land partiers enter the building. I saw a black Suburban with black tint pull up to the valet. I saw Maison exit first then Sydney. I took one look at her face and knew she was fragile and on borrowed time. Maison looked carefree and arrogant as he grabbed for Sydney's hand before entering the building. I saw Sydney look around just before walking into the building. I kept my eyes on the Suburban when the driver pulled off to park and wait for his sleazy boss to call him. The driver parked a couple blocks down from the premiere nightspot. I sat in my car thinking of how was I going to pull this off. Just then Sydney texted me.

"Ok Lance we're here. What's your plan?"

"Relax and have a drink. You just got there."

"I can't relax. He had his hand in the small of my back walking in. He wants more than a meet and greet with my client."

"Have a drink and start some light conversation about real estate."

"I'm tired of this. Make your move quickly Lance."

"You wouldn't just walk off a set would you?"

"This isn't a set. This man is real and he wants something I'm not giving him. Period!"

"Get a drink Sydney! I'll text you in a few."

"Ok! I hate you Lance!"

Sydney was becoming unraveled and I had to move quickly but cautiously or she could end up dead and my chance to grab Maison would be forever lost. I didn't see Maison's security team but it didn't mean they weren't close by. I sat and observe the flow of traffic and how many black and white squad cars rolled by. In a span of thirty minutes only one squad car drove by. I looked over at the entrance and the line had died down. The bouncers were standing around talking to each other and flirting with the women as they went in and out of SoHo. I thought about calling Townsend but time wasn't on my side or Sydney's. It was now or never. I sent Sydney a text.

"Tell him you're not feeling well and you're ready to leave. Be convincing." I said.

"Ok. What are you going to do Lance?"

"Just convince him you're ready to go and don't make a scene."

"Are you coming inside?"

"No! I'll see you outside but don't come outside looking around."

"I hate you Lance!"

"Be sure to put your seatbelt on."

"What?"

I didn't reply to her text. I made sure my 9MM had a full clip and the automatic weapon was fully loaded as well in case things got nasty. Althea sent me a text.

"How's your friend doing Lance?

"I'm glad I came. It was truly a life or death emergency. I should be home in an hour or so."

"Ok! I still may go home. I don't want you to feel rushed to get back to me."

She had no idea I was about to commit murder again and I wasn't with a friend.

"Hang out until I get back."

"Take your time. Don't worry about me."

"I'll be there before you know it."

"Get back to your friend. Sorry to bother you."

Her thoughtfulness was like nothing I'd ever experienced. It made me second guess everything. I wanted to text Sydney and tell her to tell Maison she'd catch a cab and that I would give her the balance of her money tomorrow. Tell her she didn't have to contact Maison or me ever again and wish her good luck with acting career.

"Thanks."

Sydney.

"Maison I'm not feeling well. Can you take me home please?"

"You've been on your phone so much are you fingers hurting?" he said with an attitude.

"Maison, my mother hasn't been feeling well if you must know. Now can you talk me home please?"

"Yeah right! Sure no problem."

"Thank you!"

I sat there tapping the steering wheel contemplating my next move. I saw Sydney and Maison exiting and the suburban pulling up. Sydney was still in part and didn't look around drawing attention. She smiled at the bouncers as they walked past but looked pitiful. Maison had a disappointed look on his face as he nodded to the bouncers before entering his suburban. I watched them pull onto Sunset Boulevard but I didn't immediately follow them. Althea's caring demeanor had given me pause.

I started the Charger and pulled onto Sunset Boulevard in the same direction of Maison and Sydney. I drove and scanned the streets for citizens out walking and how much traffic was on Sunset. I drove a little faster to get closer to them. I looked in the rearview to see if Maison's security team was following behind us. I didn't see anyone. The suburban was in the middle lane. I changed lanes and chambered a round in the 9MM. There were two cars in front of the suburban. I drove up to the back right wheel and hit the button for the front window to roll down. I saw Sydney entered first so she was on the opposite side of Maison. I thought about the way Maison ambushed me and left me for dead and pulled the trigger. The first shot shattered the passenger window. The driver swerved and looked at me. The next shot hit him and he lost control of the sports utility vehicle in traffic. I slowed down and the vehicle swerved from the middle lane into a parked car on Sunset. I pressed the gas pedal to the floor and pulled up to the side of the suburban. Maison was opening the back door when I pointed my 9MM at him.

"Lance!"

"Surprise!" I said.

"Sydney! Get out and get out of here."

"Sydney! What the hell?" Maison said.

"Yeah! Didn't see that coming did you?" I asked. "Move Maison"

I saw him looking around. I moved closer to him with the gun drawn and repeated myself. He walked slowly towards the Charger. Then he tried to swing at me and I stepped back.

"Maison another move like I'll end this quicker than I want to. Now move."

I saw Sydney running across the street with her cell phone up to her ear already. I didn't know who she was calling and I didn't care. I had what I wanted. I popped the trunk of the Charger and hit Maison in his head with the butt of the gun. He fell into the trunk and yelled out.

"Lance! Don't kill me." He said.

I shot him once in his each leg and slammed the trunk and ran to the driver's side. I backed up and sped up Sunset to the freeway. I didn't feel the joy I thought I would grabbing Maison. I heard him moving around in the trunk causing the car to move. I sent Althea a text.

"Are you still at my place?"

"Yes! Why?"

"I'm headed back."

"Ok. I'm going home when you get here."

"Ok. See you soon."

I slowed my speed as I approached the freeway. The radio station I was listening to interrupted the music with a special report of a shoot out in L.A. not too far from SoHo leaving one dead. The radio caster said eyewitnesses saw a black Charger leaving the scene. I didn't hear anything about a suspect but I had to get to Hollywood Hills quickly and park the Charger for good.

When I drove through the gates of my hideaway my thoughts of wanted Althea to stay had changed. As much as I enjoyed her company it was time to put Maison to rest and live the city of angels. The odds of Althea joining me were not in my favor. I drove up to the garage but didn't open it. I left the Charger outside to avoid Althea hearing my package moving around. I turned the engine off and got out cautiously looking around. I opened the trunk slightly and saw Maison still conscious and bleeding. His big eyes looked up at me in pity. I guess he was counting on the police to catch me instead me catching him first. I punched twice in face and slammed the trunk shut. When I walked towards the front door I didn't see any lights on so I wasn't sure if Althea had fallen back asleep. I unlocked the front door and walked to the living room. Althea was sitting on the sofa in the dark. I reached for the light switch on the wall and turned on the light. She turned to me slowly and stood up.

"Patrick, we need to talk."

I froze where I was standing. Thoughts of her going through the rental house and finding my money and powering up the laptops flooded my mind. Those thoughts were telling me don't answer any questions and just kill her and Maison. Don't worry about making him suffer just end it and leave. The rental was under Patrick Green's name so I'd have to see Little Red again. I'm not sure if Althea saw me move my right hand to the small of my back. I gripped the handle of the 9MM ready to kill her if the wrong question was asked.

"Hi! About what?"

"We had unprotected sex," she said.

I quietly exhaled and released the grip of my gun.

"Yes we did. Why didn't you put another condom on?"

"I got caught up in the moment."

"If you make you feel any better last check up I was disease free and I haven't had unprotected sex since then."

She looked away before speaking again.

"Patrick, I really do like you. I just feel something isn't right."

"Something like what?"

"Your body language doesn't give off a good vibe. You never seem relaxed."

"That's funny because I find myself very relax around you."

"In Santa Monica you squeezed my hand tight because you thought you saw an old business associate. Then walking to my car you rushed me along the sidewalk when you saw police speeding by. Is that normal to you?" She asked.

"I admit squeezing your hand was out of character and I shouldn't have lost my cool. The sidewalk incident was just a second nature I've developed when it comes to police in general with all of unarmed black me being killed." I lied.

"True. I will agree with you on taking precaution as a black male." Still I'm not totally comfortable."

"We are still getting to know each other. Doesn't come in time?"

"Yes it does but we've had sex a couple of times already and one of those times unprotected."

"That's an easy fix."

"How so?"

"We will use protection."

"Are you upset with me?" she asked.

"No! I was shocked but I could have stopped you just the same. Let's move on." I said walking towards her.

We hugged each other and I heard her sniffle. She was crying. I held her tightly and let her have her moment. My thoughts were on how soon I could politely get her to leave so I could do away with the trash in the trunk of the Charger. She released her embrace and kissed me.

"Patrick, you're a good person."

"So are you."

"I need to go. I should have left sooner. I'll call you when I make it home."

"Are you sure? You can stay until the sun comes up at least."

"No I'm fine."

We kissed once more then Althea turned and headed for the garage through the kitchen. I asked her again if she would like to stay, knowing I was glad she was leaving. She turned and smiled at me but kept walking to the door that opened into the garage.

"Patrick I had a really nice time. Better than I expected."

"I'm glad to hear that."

"I broke one of my own conditions." She laughed.

"We're adults. Let it go seriously"

"Ok I will and I'll call you when I get home. Will you still be up?"

"Yes! I have some work to do."

"More work on the reassessment?"

"Yes! I'm putting the final touches on it."

"I'm happy for you Patrick."

"Thank you. Don't forget to call me when you get

home."

Althea pressed the button to open the garage and took one last look at me before walking to her car.

"Why didn't you park in the garage?" She asked.

"I wasn't sure if you had fallen back asleep and I didn't want to wake you."

"You didn't think about me waking me when you left."

"That was different. You were sleeping good after a great workout." I said.

"You're so arrogant Patrick."

"I've been called worse."

"I can see why. Bye!"

Althea got into her car back out and drove to the front gate. I stepped into the garage and walked to the opening. I pressed the gate remote when she got close to the gate and watched her leave thinking would I ever see her again. After the gate closed I started the Charger up and parked inside the garage. Once the garage door was closed I opened the trunk to see Maison bleeding and unconscious. I lifted his body out of the trunk and dropped him on the floor. I kicked him in his stomach and he coughed. Looking at him lay there gave me déjà vu of how he left me for dead.

"Any last wishes?"

He coughed again before answering.

"You'll never get away with this." He said.

"I've heard that before."

"Don't you want to know about your immigrant housekeeper?"

"No! After I kill you a new life begins for me. The past is the past."

"A man like you never leaves his past. It's always in the shadows."

"Not for me. You're the last shadow I have to worry about."

"Are you sure about that? What about Jordan? Kennedy? You don't think they'll seek revenge for the grief you caused them? He asked.

"How do you know about Kennedy?"

"My daughter told me quite a bit before a coward killed her."

"She did talk a lot." I said.

"Is that why you killed her?" he asked.

"My freedom was at stake."

"You're a coward Lance. You could have let my daughter be and just left her alone."

"If I had done that I wouldn't be here right now. She had discovered too many pieces to the puzzle."

He started to whimper lying there. I left him there and ran into the house to get what I needed to end his life. I had grown tired of the useless conversation. I was angry that I wouldn't be able to torture him as I had planned. Judging from the way he was whimpering the death of Sofia had been torture enough.

When I walked back into the garage I walked over to Maison and he didn't look pitiful. He was too arrogant to accept this was the end for him. I thought about Catalina and if he really knew where she was.

"Do you know where Catalina is?" I asked.

He laughed and looked away. I lifted the 9MM and attached the silencer to it and took aim at Maison.

"Answer me Maison!"

He didn't say a word. I aimed the gun at his left arm and squeezed the trigger once. He yelled out in agony but didn't answer my question. I was beyond annoyed. I walked towards him and stood over his body with the gun pointed down at him.

"Are you going to answer me?" I asked.

"Go to hell! How's that for answer? He said.

My cell phone started buzzing in my pocket. I pulled it out and looked at the screen. It was Althea calling. I ignored the call and assumed the call meant she had made it home safely. I pointed the gun at Maison's stomach and squeezed the trigger. The bullet hit him and he made a grunting sound. A pool of blood was forming on the garage floor. I guess I wouldn't be getting my cleaning fee deposit back from the rental owner. I asked one last time about Catalina and Maison had enough strength left to laugh at me; his last laugh. I squeezed the trigger and watched the bullets hit his body repeatedly until I knew he was dead. Maison's eyes were still open but his body was lifeless. I didn't immediately feel vindicated for some reason. I walked into the house and called Althea back. She answered and sounded wide awake.

"I'm home. What were you doing when I called? Did you fall asleep?" She asked.

"No I didn't. I was finishing what we've been talking about." I said.

"That's great! Now what? What's your next move?"

"More than likely I'm going to leave L.A."

There was silence between us.

"Are you serious Patrick? Where? When?"

"Probably in a week or two.

"Where? She asked again.

"Overseas. There are some export investments opportunities I want to get into."

"And you have to be there to do that?"

"I'd rather be there than deal with the time difference."

"I forgot about that. Overseas where?"

She was really curious.

"There are a few places I'm looking at."

"There you go with the secrets again."

"There's an island named Mustique or Dubai."

"I've never heard of Mustique but I've heard of Dubai." She said.

"Are you happy now?" I was irritated.

"About what?"

"I answered your question."

"No I'm not happy. I was... I was…"

"You were what?" I asked.

"Never mind Patrick! I wish you all the best with your new move."

"Thank you! Will I be able to see you before I leave?"

She didn't respond immediately. Her disappointment evident.

"It's probably best if we don't in my opinion. I have to go Patrick." She said.

Before I could respond Althea had hung up. I was almost starting to believe that things might work out with Althea once I killed Maison. I told Althea a lie about moving. I didn't have a clue at the moment what my next move was. I knew the cops were only a few steps behind me and I had to make sure they didn't catch up to me. I knew I would be a taking a chance when I left the rental house. I had no choice but to call Townsend. I thought about calling Althea back. I didn't. She was right. It probably was not a good idea for us to see each other again. I enjoyed being with her so much and it pained me knowing I may not see her ever again. I looked around the rental home taking in the brief memories with Althea. I kept trying to convince myself that what we had was real. Maybe the only thing real about us was that I hadn't paid for sex and we had spent more than a few hours together in a hotel. Everything else was lie. How could she ever believe me? I let that question float around as I called Townsend.

He sounded half asleep when he answered.

"Yeah!"

"I didn't think you slept." I said.

"On occasion I catch a nap here and there. What's up?"

"I need you!" I told him.

"What else is new? I saw the news about a black Charger. Was that you?" he laughed.

"Yes! What's so funny?"

"I can't believe how sloppy you've gotten." He continued laughing.

"Yeah well I killed Maison. I can't risk driving the Charger anymore."

I could hear him moving around.

"You did?"

"Why do you sound surprised?" I asked.

"I didn't think you'd be able to do it."

"Well it's done. I need a car." I said.

"No you need a plane ticket!"

"I'm not leaving yet."

"Lance! You've done what you needed to do. It's time to leave L.A."

I thought his next comment would have been about Catalina, not about me leaving. Although I knew he was right. I couldn't leave yet. I needed to know if Catalina was alive or dead.

"Where is the body Lance?"

"It's here in the garage of a house I rented."

"Why in the hell did you rent a house? Never mind don't answer that. What are you going to do with the body?" He asked.

"I'm going to dump it in the ocean."

"What's the address?" He asked.

I gave him the address to the house in the hills and he told me he'd be here in an hour or less. I walked back to the garage and immediately smelled Maison's dead body. His face and hands were no longer their natural color. His skin was purple looking and the blood was dry on his suit. I stepped over him and emptied everything I had left in the Charger. I went back inside and waited for Townsend to show up. I wondered if he'd tell me about Catalina once he got here and saw the body for himself. I thought some more about Althea and if I should press the issue. The more I thought about it the more it became clearer to leave well enough alone.

Waiting for Townsend seemed like forever when I heard the bell from the front gate. I went to the security camera and it was Townsend by himself. I buzzed him and walked outside through the front door to greet him. He pulled up in a black GMC Yukon.

"How did you find this place? He asked.

"Does it really matter? Where's Catalina?" I asked.

"Lance, you don't know when to quit I see."

"Just tell me if she's alive or dead."

"She was alive last I heard."

"Last you heard? When was that?" I asked.

"When she called me." He laughed.

"So you haven't spoken to her or seen her?"

"You said tell you if she's alive or dead. Where's the body? We need to get out of here."

"Damn Townsend! It's this way." I said.

"Lance, you really need to get out of L.A. and stop worrying about your old housekeeper."

"I'll decide when it's time for me to leave."

"You're going to mess around and get caught. Who did you go on a date with?"

"Look Townsend that's not important. What is important is getting this dead body out of here like you said. So let's do that and I won't ask you about Catalina anymore."

"That's the best thing you've said since I got to L.A."

We walked into the house in silence to the garage. The smell of death had made its way into the house and it lingered. The cleaning fee deposit was definitely gone. Townsend brought black plastic with him to roll Maison's body in. The silence between us continued as we rolled Maison up. Townsend and I lifted Maison's body into the trunk of the Charger.

"So Lance what's next? Another date? More shopping? I'm just curious." He asked.

"You can stop with the insults. I'm going to find

another place for a few days then make my decision." I said.

"A few days? Man, you act like you're a law-abiding citizen. There's a massive manhunt for you. Those hunts normally don't end in the suspect's favor. You need to leave L.A. as soon as possible."

His voice was a little louder and stern this time. I looked at him as he stood there giving me what he thought was sound advice. What he was saying went in one ear and out of the other. I had to find Catalina before I left. I just had to. To Townsend I should have been grateful to be alive. Grateful that I'd killed the two people I wanted to kill. Grateful to be walking the streets instead of locked up behind bars. But I wasn't! I was anxious and empty. I felt a little pleasure killing Thad but honestly didn't feel anything when I killed Maison. My feelings had changed and killing didn't matter as much to me as finding Catalina and possibly starting a new life with Althea. It was clear Townsend would never understand and I wasn't going to try to explain it.

"One last time Townsend, do you know where Catalina is?"

He didn't answer right away. Instead he looked around the empty garage and the pool of blood on the ground. He looked at the Charger and then back at me.

"Can you open the garage so I can dump this body and get my ass back to New York? My work here is done. I wish you the best Lance. You're going to need it."

He opened the car door and proceeded to get in. I reached and grabbed his arm.

"Hey! Is that it?" I asked.

"Get your hand off of me and don't ever do that again or else there will be two bodies in the trunk."

"Just tell me where she is. I know you know."

"I'll tell you what. Purchase an airline ticket to leave L.A. with the credit card you wasted on this place and I'll think about telling you. Otherwise don't ask me again. Now open the garage so I can go."

If looks could kill Townsend would be that other body in the trunk. He returned the stare with no words spoken. After a few seconds I pressed the button to open the garage door. Townsend started up the Charger and backed out. I opened the gate for him to drive out and didn't wait for it to close. Something about our last exchange of words told me it would be a long time before I saw my friend again. I walked back in the house and gathered my things to put inside my new mode of transportation. I turned off all of the lights inside the house and locked the front door. I started the SUV and sat there for a moment. I thought about my very first kill. The feeling was similar to how I felt tonight after I killed Maison; numb. This time the numbness was different. The numbness I felt years ago was out of fear and recklessness to convince myself I could do this for a living. But tonight I felt nothing, not even an inkling of joy after killing the bastard that left me for dead. Maybe I should have died that night. Maybe I should turn myself in and begin a new life of rehabilitating inside prison. Maybe I should go to Althea's condo and tell her that I love her and that my past isn't exactly stellar but it's behind me now and I want to live my life loving somebody; that somebody being her. Tell her that she gave me the air to breathe and believe in unconditional love. Something I'd never experienced before. All of these thoughts went through my mind in the dawn of the night.

I drove to the front gate and hit the remote to open it. When I got outside of the gate, I got out of the SUV and took one last look at the house where memories were made and they weren't from a random person with an online profile and an hourly rate. Althea was as real as they come. Her personality was beautiful and kind. I enjoyed her company and we laughed together. None of it was staged and paid for. After a few minutes of smiling I walked to the lockbox and input the code that I received in an email. I opened it and put the house keys and two remotes back inside. Just before closing it I said thank you silently then pressed it shut and got back in the SUV.

When I left Hollywood Hills I didn't know where I was headed but I couldn't stay on the streets too long. Something inside me was saying I should call Sydney and see how she was doing but I couldn't bring myself to do it. She had done her part and all we needed to discuss was the remaining half of her money. That could be done via text message. I hit the freeway and let the sounds of the Sirius station watercolors drown out my thoughts. I watched the digital reading in the SUV to avoid a highway patrol pulling me over. I didn't want to kill anyone else, at least not tonight.

I ended up in the city of Burbank not too far from the Burbank airport. I checked into a Marriott hotel as Patrick Green. I parked in the self-park garage. This time I wasn't nervous when I checked in. I wasn't looking over my shoulder anymore. It was as if I wanted someone to turn me in to free my soul. I didn't feel myself anymore after seeing Townsend. When he didn't tell me if Catalina was alive or dead I felt something leave me. Townsend was right in saying I had done what I needed to do but all of it didn't matter at this point with the uncertainty of Catalina. The front desk representative interrupted my thoughts and told me all of the things on the checklist for guests checking in. I had heard it so many times I could have interrupted her and not skipped a beat. When she was done, all I remember her saying was my room number and where the elevators were before handing me the room key card. I was courteous and told her thank you before walking towards the elevators. I walked into the room and dropped my things on the floor and plopped down on the bed. I didn't turn on the TV or any lights. I could hear airplanes landing at the nearby airport. The darkness gave me a calming feeling I hadn't felt in a long time.

I stayed on the bed and didn't shower. I don't remember when I fell asleep but when I woke up it was close to 1 o'clock in the afternoon. I looked at my phone and I didn't have any text messages or missed calls from Althea or Townsend. I sat up in the bed and immediately smelt the fresh sheets mixed in with the odor of yesterday on me. I got up and went to the bathroom to shower. I didn't bother looking in the mirror, I knew what I looked like and the story my face would tell. It was an unhappy story I knew all too well and wanted a change. The constant sounds of airplanes descending really put the idea of leaving into my immediate thoughts. The hot shower felt so good and I wished the water splashing against my body had the power to baptize me and make me a born again man.

After I dried off and got dressed I ordered room service and turned on the TV. Like all of the other channels I'd seen, a newscaster was reporting on me still being at large. I searched the guide and found a college basketball game while I waited for my lunch. A few minutes later I heard a knock at the door. I didn't ask who was it or reach for my 9MM before opening the door. The young employee was chipper as he rushed in with the table cart holding my food. He removed the cover from my Salmon salad, pointed to the salad dressing and the coke I ordered then presented the bill to me for my signature. I grabbed the pen and starting signing as Lance Goodman but caught myself and made the L into a P and continue to sign as the guest that checked in downstairs. I sat looking out of the window as I ate my lunch.

As planes approached the airport, I thought of a destination I could retreat to and start over. The island of Curacao kept circling in my head. I didn't know much about it but I had seen a special on it years ago, and the island looked relaxing and a place of peace. The primary language was Dutch but English was spoken there as well.

Perhaps I could start a charter or fishing boat venture and meet lots of exciting people. I finished my lunch and powered up my laptop to look into residency in Curacao.

Before I started exploring my future hideaway I called Althea.

"Hello!"

"Hi! How are you?" I asked.

"I'm well Patrick. What about you?"

"That's a good question. Thanks for asking."

"I thought you'd feel better after your reassessment and the decision you've made." She said.

"I thought I would too but something doesn't feel right."

"What do you mean?"

"Well I was hoping to get some clarity afterwards."

"And you don't have any?" she asked.

"Not really." I said.

Althea remained silent and didn't lend any advice.

"Althea......"

"Yes Patrick!"

"Can we meet for lunch one day this week? I need to see you." I asked.

She didn't reply as quick as I would have liked.

"I'm not sure. This coming week will be busy with the

untimely death of that police officer I told you about. Besides I don't really see the point." She said.

"Okay but if you could make time I'd appreciate it."

She was right and I knew it. Meeting for lunch or anything for that matter was a moot point. Something was definitely different about me. I actually sounded like I cared and needed her.

"I will do that Patrick." She said.

"Thanks."

"I need to go. I'm sure you have lots to do before your big move."

"You're right. I just powered up my laptop."

"Talk to you later. Goodbye!" She said.

"Bye!"

My high expectations were quickly shattered. Althea responded just how I figured she would; cold. I typed in the island of Curacao in the search space and began to read the fact section of the island. The pictures looked very pretty and judging from the pictures and the information I read I felt I could make it there and not worry about my real identity being revealed. I opened another tab and searched for private chartered flights leaving from Burbank ten days from today. I still held on to a glimmer of hope to hear about Catalina. If she was alive and still wanted to be around me I'd take her with me. I booked the flight and put my laptop away. I sent Townsend a text message asking for Little Red's phone number. I needed a passport to match the ID I had in my possession. He called me instead of replying to the text. I didn't want to talk to him to be honest. I don't think either one of us were ready to have a serious conversation.

"Hello!" I said.

"What do you need Little Red's number for? He doesn't know you."

"I need two passports."

"Two?" He asked.

"Yes, in case Catalina is still alive."

"You think she'll just fly away freely with you?"

"Only one way to find out. Are you going to give me the contact information?" I asked.

"No I'm not. I can tell him what you need and get it to you."

"Why not? I can handle this. I don't need you."

"Do you want me to get the passports or not?"

"Yeah whatever!"

"Look you're a grown man, get them yourself from another source then."

"Just get the passports for me Townsend."

"You can check the attitude. I don't work for you and the friendship we have won't last much longer if you keep coming at me like this."

"When can I expect to have the passports?" I asked.

"I don't know. I'll contact you when I have them. Again, I don't work for you Lance!" He said.

I knew this conversation wasn't going to go well but I couldn't remember where Little Red lived and his work was great so I needed Townsend. Damn that pained me to call him. I simply told Townsend thanks and hung up the phone.

It looked like a beautiful day outside and I wished I could be outside walking around freely but I knew every time I stepped outside it was a risk. I kept the drapes open and relaxed in the bed and channel surfed the TV the rest of the day. I napped in between two movies on the Turner Network. It was dark outside and the airplane lights were steadily coming in from the east and I saw a little traffic down on the streets. I pulled out the menu to order room service again when my cell phone buzzed. I rushed over to the desk hoping it was Althea. It was Sydney.

"Hello!" I said.

"When do I get the rest of my money?" she asked.

I wasn't expecting the harsh greeting.

"Are you available now?" I asked.

"Yes I am. Where would you like to meet?"

"Yard House in Pasadena."

"What time?"

"The sooner the better." I said.

"I'll be there in an hour." She said.

I hung up without saying goodbye. I was glad Sydney called and was anxious to close this chapter in both of our lives. I put the menu away and jumped in the shower. After I showered and got dressed I unzipped the duffle bag and pulled out the rest of Sydney's money.

When I got downstairs the lobby was busy and a live band was playing in the bar area. My trip to Pasadena was going to be quick. I will take in the live music when I got back. I walked through the lobby towards the parking garage and didn't pay attention to anyone and it didn't feel like anyone noticed me. Before I walked to the SUV I looked around the garage to see if anything looked out of the ordinary. More people had checked in after me and the parking garage had more cars. I pulled the 9MM from the small of my back and got in the SUV. I got on the freeway for the quick ride to Pasadena. I wanted to arrive earlier to see if Sydney was bringing company with her. Maybe she had worked out a special deal of her own with the L.A.P.D.

I parked on Colorado Street and enjoyed watching the people out and about. All walks of life came through the city of Pasadena and it was something or someone guaranteed to get your attention. I saw Sydney pull up in front of the Yard House and valet park. I didn't see any cars that looked like they may have been following her. I stayed in the SUV until I saw her walk into the restaurant. I waited to see if someone would follow her in. No one walked in behind her and I didn't see any dark color vans or unmarked cars near the restaurant. I got out of the SUV and proceeded to the restaurant. I walked Colorado Street like I was a free man without a care in the world. I saw two cops walking the sidewalk but I didn't adjust my cap or shy away. I kept walking and as I got closer to them I even extended a greeting. They nodded and kept moving up the block.

Inside the restaurant, I saw Sydney sitting at the crowded bar area. A big 10 basketball game was showing on all of the TV screens. I walked up to Sydney and tapped her on her shoulder. She turned around holding a mixed drink in her hand. I extended my hand into her rib area with her money. She felt the nudge and looked down then she looked around the restaurant before taking the money out of my hand. I turned around and walked away before she could speak. This was the end of a relationship that ended well for both parties. I'm certain that if I hadn't left Althea at the house when I did, Sydney wouldn't have been able to keep it together and Maison would have killed her. I thought I heard her whisper something but I didn't break my stride towards the entrance of the restaurant. I made it back to the SUV and as I drove past the restaurant I saw Sydney standing outside looking around. I didn't slow my speed or stop. I kept towards the freeway to get back to Burbank. Driving on the freeway I received a text message from Sydney.

Why did you leave so abruptly?

I didn't reply and deleted the message. Soon after another message came in thanking me for everything and wishing me safety. Again I hit delete and didn't reply.

The hotel was still lively when I walked back into the lobby. I grabbed a seat at the bar and ordered a double shot of Macallan 25 on the rocks. The bartender placed my drink in front of me and I didn't waste any time. I downed it like it was water. It was so smooth going down. I ordered another. I sat there and listened to the live band playing songs from the 80s and 90s. The lead singer was a taller than average female that favored Sheila E. My cell phone buzzed. I hope it wasn't Sydney. Althea had sent a text message.

Hi Patrick! I've been thinking. Meeting you for lunch isn't a good idea. I hope you understand and I wish you all the best on your new ventures. Take care, Althea.

Now I wish the text had been from Sydney. Her message didn't mean anything but this one meant everything. I felt like my body melted into a liquid form and rolled down the bar stool onto the floor as everyone stepped on me. Althea sealed the little faith I had in ever seeing her again. She was removing herself from whatever we had started and politely telling me not to contact her again. I sat there reading the brief but powerful text message repeatedly. I didn't even hear the bartender trying to get my attention. The message couldn't have been any clearer. I finally asked the bartender for another double. When he brought this one back I stepped away from the bar and walked to a nearby sitting area. I couldn't stop reading Althea's text message. I pressed the telephone icon to call her even though her text message was clear. I wanted her in my life so bad. I had to have her in my life. Our brief time together had meant the world to me and I didn't want it to stop. I wanted her to understand why I lied and to forgive me and to give us a chance. Her number was now on the screen and all I had to do was press the green button to connect. I didn't press it right away. I looked around the hotel lobby and saw people going about their business, happy and some full of libations. I downed my double shot of Mac 25 and pressed the button to call Althea.

"Hello!"

"Hi!" I said in a slurred voice.

"Patrick?" she asked.

"Yes, it's me. Can we talk?"

"You've made your decision to leave the country so I don't think there's much to talk about. Where are you? It's loud." She said.

"I'm out listening to some music. What if I've changed my mind?"

"We're too old to play the 'what if' game Patrick."

"It's not a game. I need you Althea."

"You need me? You need me how? You're not making any sense. Have you been drinking?" She asked.

"Yes, I have but I'm not drunk and I'm aware of what I'm saying. Yes, I need you."

"Patrick there seems to be too many missing pieces in

your life."

"I know. That was all part of the reassessment. So I could start a new life. I want that new life with you Althea."

"How are you so sure?"

"I've never experienced what you give me."

"I haven't given you anything. Well, we've had sex a couple of times and been out twice. What have I given you Patrick?"

"I feel alive when I'm with you. When I'm not with you I'm wondering what you're doing. It has nothing to do with sex."

"Patrick I don't know what to say. When you said you were moving it didn't seem like I meant anything to you at all."

"I can't tell you why I made it seem that way. All I can tell you is I don't want to be without you."

"Patrick I need some time and you've been drinking. You may wake up in the morning and not remember any of this. I need some space. I have to go. Goodbye."

And just like that Althea hung up without giving me any more time to try and convince her. I hadn't told any woman that I needed her. Up until now I could care less about a woman, her needs or her emotions. Somehow my selfishness died at the same time Maison took his last breath and Althea was the first person to know of my revelation. I had done so much evil that love didn't give a damn about my feelings. I needed to ask for forgiveness before I could ask someone to forgive me. I sat there in the hotel lobby feeling sorry for myself and wishing someone would walk by and recognize me from the TV and turn me in. I wanted another drink. In fact, I wanted several to drown my sorrow away. I stood up and walked more like stumbled to the bar and asked for another double Mac 25. The bartender knew I didn't need another but he must have felt my pain because he brought me another double but told me this was it and he'd get me some coffee if I wanted anything else. I looked at him in a drunken stare and lifted the glass and downed it. Then slammed the glass on the counter. I made it to the elevator and was able to push my floor. I inserted the key card into the slot to my room and opened the door. After I walked into my room I collapsed on the floor just as the door closed.

I woke up the next morning in extreme pain from sleeping on the floor all night. I sat up and looked around the room. I was alone and no one else had been there. I looked at my cell phone and I didn't have any missed calls. The last text message received was the one from Althea. I could hear airplane taking off and landing and I saw the bright sun rising. I freshened up before going downstairs for breakfast. The lobby looked deserted compared to last night. I didn't see the bartender and I was glad because I had embarrassed myself. I walked into the restaurant and one of the waitresses told me I could seat myself. I found a table by the window and facing the entrance of the restaurant. When I sat down I pulled out my cell phone and called Althea. Her phone went straight to voicemail. I didn't leave a message. I ordered a southwestern omelet and had a cup of coffee. When I got back to my room I laid across the bed feeling drained. The thought of staying in L.A. for ten days without seeing or talking to Althea made me want to change my travel plans but I still wanted to find out about Catalina. I knew I shouldn't keep taking the risk of walking the streets so I decided I would stay in the hotel until it was time for me to depart.

The first week in the hotel was tough. I watched so many reruns on TV and had become bored hearing about my manhunt. I watched a few basketball games but all of the NBA teams were struggling in my opinion. No one stood out as a dominating team to be world champions. The build up to the inauguration was beyond amusing. I'm not sure how America let a celebrity become the leader of the free world. It should be an interesting 4 years. Townsend kept his word and delivered a new passport with the name Patrick Green on it. He gave me a passport for Catalina but he didn't mention Catalina and neither did I. Althea hadn't called or text me which made the days that much longer. I was on a first name basis with the hotel staff. The live band hadn't played since the night I melted like putty.

The sun was starting to set as I finished my workout in the hotel gym when my cell phone buzzed. It was Althea. I immediately sat down on the weight bench and answered.

"Hello!"

"Hi Patrick! It's Althea."

"How are you?" I asked.

"I've seen better days. Is this a bad time for you?" she asked.

"No, it's not. What's wrong?"

"Going against my text message, I would like to meet with you. Can I come over?"

"I'm not at home. When did you want to meet?" I asked.

"Tonight."

"Tonight? Where? What time?" I asked.

"No place fancy. Can you meet me at the Starbucks on

Crenshaw Boulevard and Coliseum Street?"

"Sure! What time?" I asked.

"How soon can you get there?" She asked.

"I'll head there now." I said.

"Okay! See you there."

Althea hung up and my heart was pounding a thousand beats per second. I had to calm myself down. I hadn't ever felt this anxious to see any woman. What made her call after a week? Had she reconsidered giving us a try? Was she going to move with me? I'd have to tell her that I wasn't moving to Dubai but to Curacao instead. I didn't go up to the room to shower or freshen up. I left the gym and headed to the parking garage. I had pep in my step as I walked towards the SUV. I could feel a slight grin on my face. Hearing her voice put me back together again. I was excited to see her. I could see her face and warm smile. I could hear her confident voice and see her alluring walk. I started the SUV and headed to the Leimert park area.

I pulled into the parking lot of Starbucks and didn't see Althea's car. I checked my phone to see if maybe she had texted or called to tell me she changed her mind. She hadn't. I parked and went inside to wait for her. Inside the coffee house it was a little busy but not crazy. I was able to find a small sofa so I sat down and waited for Althea to arrive. I saw her walk in looking for me. I got her attention and she walked over to where I was sitting. When she got closer I stood up and extended my arms to hug her but she didn't let me. She gently grabbed my arms and pushed them down and smiled before sitting down.

"Thanks for meeting me Patrick. This isn't going to take too long." She said.

"Okay what's wrong?" I asked.

She was fidgeting with the bottom of her lightweight jacket and looking around the coffee house.

"Althea!" I repeated my question.

"This is a bad idea." She finally said.

"What's going on?" I asked again.

Now she was looking directly at me with a blank stare and still fidgeting. I heard her exhale. Then she looked around the coffee house again.

"Patrick! Why did you lie to me? She asked.

I slump my head down before answering.

"What did I lie about?" I asked.

"Well for starters your name isn't Patrick, is it?"

I looked around the coffee house to see if Althea had brought the police with her. Everyone in there was enjoying their coffee or latte and not worried about me. I cleared my throat before attempting to answer.

"Let me explain Althea."

"Explain what? That you're a murderer and God knows what else you're into. It's certainly not laundromats." She said.

I felt the tension and couldn't downplay the moment.

"I'm not a murderer Althea."

"Just stop it. I was so busy with my own case workload that I hadn't looked at the news too much so I didn't recognize you at the gas station. But when the sketch artist drew the description of the man the eyewitness saw firing into the car Thad was killed in, it hit me hard like a sledgehammer." She said.

I stood up and began to walk away.

"Sit down Patrick, I mean...I don't know who to call you." She said.

A few people looked around and noticed the uncomfortable situation. I kept standing looking down at Althea. She looked up at me and told me to sit down again with a stern voice.

"Look I don't want to be here but but... I'm pregnant Patrick!" she said.

"What?" I asked.

"You heard me. I feel like an idiot." She said.

I saw a tear roll down her left cheek.

"Althea it's ok, we'll be fine." I said.

"Are you serious? We won't be fine." She raised her voice. "You're on your way to prison and I have to decide if I'm keeping the child of a murderer."

"Don't kill our baby!" I pleaded.

"This is my child and I'll decide what I'm going to do."

Her attitude was ever present.

"Althea, let's leave L.A. and raise our child together overseas." I said.

"Overseas? My parents wouldn't like that. Wait a minute, why am I even considering any of this? You're wanted for murder and eventually you'll be caught. I'm not living my life on the run with you."

"Why don't you turn me in then Althea?" I asked.

"I thought about it when I asked you to meet me but..."

"But what? You love me?"

"You really are crazy! I don't know anything about you. I'm so ashamed. No I don't love you."

"You didn't feel so ashamed when you had unprotected sex with me."

She stood up and slapped me. "Asshole!"

"I apologize. I shouldn't have said that." I said.

"You shouldn't have done a lot of things Patrick."

"Althea, you having this baby would mean so much to me. Don't get an abortion." I pleaded.

"You'll be in prison. What's so special about a child seeing his father through a plate of glass? He or she wouldn't even be able to touch you, kiss you or hug you. I'm getting pissed. I'm pretty sure I'm not having this baby."

I reached to grab her hand but she pulled it away and told me not to touch her. I looked around the coffee house and a few people were looking and pointing at us now. I was starting to feel uncomfortable and wondered if someone recognized me.

"Patrick, we should get out of here."

"Are we going to your place?" I asked.

"No, we're not going to my place. When do you leave for your new location? Your hideaway?" She asked.

"I leave in three days."

"This is just so unbelievable and so unlike me."

"We're adults and we made an adult decision." I said.

"Is that your pep talk before you kill your victim."

I was getting annoyed with her calling me a murderer. I didn't need the reminder. I was going to be a father. My DNA was now connected to another life. I'm going to be responsible for another life; a little person that hopefully one day will look up to me. I wouldn't be like my sperm donor, emotionally detached and irresponsible. None of these wonderful thoughts mattered if Althea was going through with the abortion. I grabbed her hand tight enough before she could pull it back and headed towards the entrance to exit. When we got outside Althea jerked her hand away from mine. I didn't reach back for her hand because I didn't need a situation to develop on Crenshaw Boulevard and have the cops roll up on us. We stood there in silence looking everywhere but at each other.

"Look Patrick I have to go. I will try to call you before you leave. I don't know if I'll have an answer regarding the baby. Don't bother calling or texting me please."

I didn't respond as she turned to walk away. I watched her walk away and thought about following her to her place and kidnapping her or killing her. I wanted her to have our baby. If she wasn't having our baby, she'd be better off dead as far as I was concerned. I didn't want a long distance relationship with my kid.

I walked back to the SUV and pulled out onto Crenshaw Boulevard behind Althea. I don't know if she knew I was following her but I stayed a few cars back in a different lane. I followed her a few more blocks before I turned down another street and parked. My mind was starting to take over in a bad way and things wouldn't have ended well for her if I had continued to follow her. I hope to hear from her before I leave. Maybe I should stay if she decides to keep the baby and take a huge risk of being captured. It was clear that Althea didn't want to be with me, so how would I see the baby? Would she even allow me to see the baby? What if she moved to San Francisco with her parents? All of these questions flooded my mind as I sat parked.

I arrived back to my hotel room and ordered room service. As I waited for my dinner to arrive I thought about everything that just happened. Althea now knew my real identity. She is pregnant and not sure if she's keeping the baby. I need to decide what I'm going to do about leaving. That decision depended on Althea's decision. I wasn't used to having my fate decided by another person, a woman at that. Althea's pregnancy really means everything to me. It's important that she know I would do anything for her and the baby despite our short courtship. She didn't give me the impression she felt the same or cared. As much as I wanted to contact her I would respect her demand and patiently wait to hear back from her. I heard a knock at the door. It was one of the hotel staff with my room service order. A young freckled face boy rolled the cart in and asked me where would I like it? I told him right in front of the desk would be fine. I signed the bill and gave him a tip. I finished my dinner and showered then I laid across the bed and watched TV until I fell asleep.

The next couple of days I did my same routine of breakfast and lunch in the hotel restaurant and ordered room service for dinner. I worked out in the hotel gym and didn't leave the premises. I didn't call Althea and I hadn't heard from her. I was all caught up on world events and was prepared for my trip to Curacao with or without Althea and Catalina. I woke up the day of my departure feeling better than I thought I would. I wasn't angry at Althea. How could I be? I was in this position because of the choices I made and I had to deal with the consequences of those choices. I never thought the consequences would be having a child I'd never see by a woman I barely knew. The relationships more than transaction I had been in were safe and secure from accidental pregnancies happening.

I gathered up my few belongings and looked around the last American style hotel I'd see in a long time and closed the door. As the elevator descended to the ground floor, I started to smile thinking how my life had changed. I wasn't in police custody handcuffed to a hospital bed. I had met a dynamic young lady who was carrying my child. It wasn't exactly the fairy tale way most couples experience. Hell, we weren't even a couple. I saw my best friend who I hadn't seen in years and he hadn't changed one bit. Although our last conversation wasn't the best I still felt the bond was strong. Along the way I lost contact with Catalina, someone who loved me better than my paternal mother ever did. In the end I couldn't be upset for not having more. I didn't deserve more. When I parked the SUV in the parking lot for my chartered flights I made sure I had everything with me. I wiped down the steering wheel, the gear shift and the arm rest and left the keys on the floor board and didn't lock the door. The Burbank terminal was much different than the Hawthorne terminal. Burbank was busier and less friendly. The lady working the counter wasn't polite at all but I was numb to everything at this point. I gave her my ID and she told me what gate door I would walk out of when my aircraft was ready. I walked over to the seating area and sat down. There were a few men standing around in jeans and sports coats talking about the L.A. Clippers and how they should move to Anaheim. They must have been Lakers fans.

I heard my name called for departure so I stood up and proceeded to the designated door. When I walked outside, a young man was waiting for me in a black sedan. We pulled up to the chartered carrier and I could see two flight attendants waiting at the bottom of the steps. I thanked the driver and headed to the airplane.

"Good evening Mr. Green! I'm Melanie and this is Leslie. We will be your flight attendants to Curacao."

"Hello!" I said.

"Please follow us."

"Thank you."

When I got to the top of the stairs I could see the mountains and a hazy looking downtown L.A. I took the scene in for a few minutes before going to my seat. Melanie took my duffle bag and stored it in a small cabinet.

"Would you like something to drink?" Leslie asked.

"A double shot of Scotch please."

"Sure Sir."

Leslie returned with my drink and told me we'd be taking off soon. Instead of downing the Scotch like I did in the hotel I enjoyed it. I heard the engines start up and I saw Melanie and Leslie smile at me as they took their seats and fastened their seat belts. I returned the smile and looked out of my window. I heard the pilot say 'we're clear for takeoff' and my cell phone buzzed. I almost spilt my drink trying to get it out of my pocket. I looked at the screen, it was Althea calling.

"Mr. Green, your cell phone needs to be powered off or in airplane mode." Leslie said.

"I really need to take this call." I said.

"We've been cleared for takeoff Mr. Green. Please power your cell phone off. Thank you."

I continued watching the screen flash until it went to voicemail. I powered off my cell phone and finished my Scotch as I felt the jet taking off.

ABOUT THE AUTHOR

Bestselling Author James H. Waggoner is a Southern California native, born in Los Angeles. He attended the University of Maryland where he earned a degree in Management Studies. James served in the U.S. Air Force for 20 years and has lived in 12 different countries. James writes his nail biting stories to capture avid readers from the first page and keep them on the edge of their seats until the end. His vivid imagination brings the characters on the page to real life. His stories are sure to give you passion, love, hate, heart beating action and a deep message to ponder long after you've finished reading his latest masterpiece.

James is active in his community with youth sports as a youth sports basketball coach and mentor. James has been a featured author and panelist at the National Book Club Conference sharing his experiences as a self- published author. He is a proud member of Omega Psi Phi Fraternity, Inc. When he's not writing, you will find James spending time with his family and friends, traveling, golfing or enjoying a fine cigar. He resides in Northern Virginia.

CONTACT

Email: authorjameshwaggoner@gmail.com

Web: www.jameshwaggoner.net

Facebook:

https://www.facebook.com/EmptySoulForHire/?fref=ts

Amazon: http://amzn.to/2kGYYLa

Thank you for reading my book. I would be most grateful if you would leave a review.

Amazon: http://amzn.to/2kGYYLa

James.